the ONE that i want

For more romantic reads
by Jennifer Echols, don't miss:

Endless Summer

Winter's Kiss

Major Crush

Forget You

Going Too Far

Love Story

Jennifer Echols

Simon Pulse

New York London Toronto Sydney New Delhi

SIMON PULSE

An imprint of Simon & Schuster Children's Publishing Division

1230 Avenue of the Americas, New York, NY 10020

First Simon Pulse paperback edition February 2012

For information about special discounts for bulk purchases, please contact Simon & Schuster Special Sales at 1-866-506-1949 or business@simonandschuster.com.

The Simon & Schuster Speakers Bureau can bring authors to your live event. For more information or to book an event contact the Simon & Schuster Speakers Bureau at 1-866-248-3049 or visit our website at www.simonspeakers.com.

Designed by Mike Rosamilia

The text of this book was set in Garamond 3.

Manufactured in the United States of America

2 4 6 8 10 9 7 5 3

Library of Congress Cataloging-in-Publication Data

Echols, Jennifer.

The one that I want / Jennifer Echols.

p. cm.

Summary: "Gemma can't believe her luck when the star football player starts flirting with her. Max is totally swoon-worthy, and even gets her quirky sense of humor. So when he asks out her so-called best friend Addison, Gemma's heartbroken. Then Addison pressures Gemma to join the date with one of Max's friends. But the more time they all spend together, the harder Gemma falls for Max. She can't help thinking that Max likes her back—it's just too bad he's already dating Addison. How can Gemma get the guy she wants without going after her best friend's boyfriend?" — Provided by publisher.

ISBN 978-1-4424-5236-7 (pbk.)

[1. Dating (Social customs)—Fiction. 2. Best friends—Fiction. 3. Friendship—Fiction. 4. High schools—Fiction. 5. Schools—Fiction. 6. Self-esteem—Fiction. 7. Drum majorettes—Fiction.] I. Title.

PZ7.E1967One 2012

[Fic]—dc23

2011041702

ISBN 978-1-4424-4193-4 (eBook)

This book is for Amy and Jessica.
It has been a long time since they were majorettes,
but when I told them I needed their expertise,
they knew exactly *where their batons were.*

Acknowledgments

Many thanks to my brilliant editor, Annette Pollert; my incomparable agent, Laura Bradford; and as always, my critique partners, Victoria Dahl and Catherine Chant, who cheered me on with every chapter of this book.

1

April

As I opened my locker, an envelope fell toward me with *Gemma* written in Robert's tight scrawl. My majorette tryout was in ten minutes. He must have known I would stop here to dump my books and grab my batons before I ran down to the gym. For two years we'd been sending each other Grandparents Day cards on our birthdays and Halloween cards on Christmas. Now he had left me this St. Patrick's Day or Father's Day card to wish me good luck.

My heart had already been pounding with anticipation of the tryouts. It jacked into overdrive at the sight of the card. Robert hadn't wanted me to try out for majorette.

He'd said I wouldn't make it. That I was the wrong type of girl. That everybody in school would make fun of me. I had hung with the artsy crowd my freshman and sophomore years of high school. He'd said that by trying out, I was admitting that I'd wanted to be part of the golden crowd after all. That I was a fraud, and I deserved what I got.

At least, that's what he'd *said.* What I'd been afraid he'd *meant* was, *You are too fat.*

I had listened to his harsh words since November, when I'd signed up to try out. His card meant that at the eleventh hour, he'd changed his mind and decided to support me. Maybe—crossing fingers—he'd finally started to see me not as a sexless friend, but as romantic material.

Just as I'd seen him the whole time.

Grinning, I slipped the card out of the envelope.

It was a sympathy card.

Okay, it was a sympathy card on the *outside.* That didn't mean he wasn't wishing me good luck on the *inside.* With shaking fingers, I opened the card.

Inside, Robert had crossed out the inspirational advice for coping with a loved one's death. Underneath, he'd scribbled:

Congratulations on giving in to the American culture of bourgeois capitalism that markets eternal emaciation and youth.
Your friend,
Robert

After the initial wave of fury, I wasn't sure what was more unbelievable: that Robert had sent me a sympathy card, or that he had signed it *Your friend*.

I talked myself down. He'd thought I would find this card as funny as he did. He was wrong, but I couldn't dwell on it. The hall was full of people jogging downstairs to see *me*. I grabbed my batons, slammed my locker door, and tossed the card into the nearest trash can. Then I stepped into the tide of humanity and got swept toward the gym.

"Gemma! Why do you have all three of your batons?" Addison hissed as I skittered into my place in line outside the gym door. We were twenty wannabes trying out for six open spots to be majorettes with the marching band next year.

The statistics were cruel enough. But even worse, rather than a panel of judges picking us on the merits of our figure eights and vertical spins in the privacy of a closed room, we had to perform our routines in front of the whole school. Every girl who'd ever taunted me for eating more than my share of Girl Scout cookies and every boy who'd ever made fun of me for driving a train with a huge caboose would decide who made the cut and who was a Loser.

Worst of all, even though I'd lost thirty pounds in the past five months, I was still the heaviest girl trying out.

I was under a little stress. And my so-called best friend Addison picked *now* to quiz me on how I set up my baton routine? She had badgered me into trying out with her in the first place.

"Last-minute change," I whispered back. It was a lie. I had planned to use three batons in my individual routine since November. Anticipating that she'd copy whatever I did and then tell everybody *I'd* copied *her*, I'd performed a dull routine whenever we'd practiced together. I'd kept my real routine supersecret.

"Well, do you want me to sit in front of you and hand you the extra batons when you need them?" Addison asked, making even her whisper sound hurt.

"No, thanks. I've got the pickups planned." I'd engineered them carefully, anticipating every disaster. If I started by twirling baton number one, placing two and three at the edge of the gym floor where I could dive for them at the appropriate points in my routine, mean boys would kick them underneath the bleachers so I couldn't reach them. For this reason, most girls had friends who would sit off to the side and hand them batons, as Addison was suggesting. These girls obviously trusted their best friends not to sabotage their routines by letting the batons roll away "accidentally."

I did not trust Addison. My batons would wait right beside me in the middle of the floor. I might trip over them, but that would be better than someone else tripping me. At least I would be in control.

Inside the gym, the voice of the principal, Ms. Zuccala, escalated in the microphone, probably announcing, "Let the games begin!" like we were gladiators about to be thrown to the lions. I couldn't hear what she really said because the gym exploded into a deafening roar of screams, whistles, applause, and feet stomping the bleachers. Majorettes were a big deal at our high school. Also, everybody was really happy to be skipping calculus.

In front of me, Delilah bounced on her toes. I had a few classes and band with her, but she was quiet, and I'd never had a conversation with her until we started majorette tryout meetings. The first thing I'd learned about her was that she was prone to panic attacks, though she was petite and beautiful and had a lot less reason to be nervous than I did. I leaned forward to whisper in her ear, "Good luck!"

She looked over her shoulder at me. "Thanks, Gemma.

You too!" she said through the tooth-baring majorette grin she'd already pasted on her face.

Then I turned to Addison, who was not beautiful but faked it well. Her makeup was model-perfect. She'd bleached her hair several shades blonder than natural and flat-ironed it into submission until it didn't dare curl in the Georgia humidity. "Good luck!" I told her.

She flared her nostrils. "Thanks," she said, half smiling, still puzzling at my three batons. When she was not privy to every detail of my life, she felt betrayed. She would not forget this.

I ignored a pang of guilt. She had betrayed me first. Our moms had been majorettes together at this high school. We'd been ten years old when Addison's mom told my mom that Addison wanted to take baton lessons, but only if a friend would take lessons with her. Wouldn't I take lessons too? I hadn't wanted to be the heaviest girl in that group either. But my mom had asked me, "You don't want Addison to miss out on something she wants to do, do you?"

Five years of baton lessons later, Addison had decided that both of us would try out for majorette. I had told her not *no* but *hell no*. She'd asked me, "Why in the world not, Gemma? Every girl at our school wants to be a majorette, and you're so much better at baton than a lot of them." And when that didn't convince me, as she knew it wouldn't, because I was not a person who did stuff just because other people were doing it, she'd asked with her usual tact, "It's the sequined leotard you'd have to wear during football games, isn't it? You're letting your weight hold you back. If you refuse to try out for majorette, you're admitting that you have a serious problem."

The prospect of dancing in front of the entire school had forced me to lose the weight Addison had been bugging me about the entire time we'd been friends. So here I was, thirty pounds lighter. We wore T-shirts and shorts to try out, thank God. I still wasn't ready for the sequined leotard. Luckily, I didn't have a chance of making the majorette squad. I would have loved Robert's support, but he was right that my effort was futile. Majorette tryouts were a popularity contest, and I was not popular.

Mrs. Baxter, the majorette coach, guarded the door into the gym. She was grandma old. She was thin, but the skin underneath her chin wobbled when she moved, in time with the jeweled chain hanging from the spectacles perched on her nose. She'd been the coach when my mother was a majorette. Mrs. Baxter had been a majorette herself several centuries ago. She ran our school's twirler line like she was stuck in time, and she always held her head perfectly level as if she were wearing a tiara.

As each girl approached her, she looked the girl over one last time, smoothed her hair or tucked a loose end of her T-shirt into her shorts, and sent her inside the gym amid renewed whoops from the student body. Mrs. Baxter looked Delilah over and didn't see anything wrong. She just put her hands lightly on Delilah's cheeks, so as not to smear Delilah's heavy makeup, and said, "You will do great. Good luck!" Delilah stepped over the threshold, into the Roman coliseum.

Mrs. Baxter turned to me.

Blinked at my hair. The guidelines for tryouts had specified that we needed to be "in full hair," which translated apparently as "big hair." My usual style was to wear my long brown hair straight with purple streaks. I was pleasantly surprised that I was able to create movie-star hair easily. Long ringlets cascaded around my shoulders. I'd even worn a rhinestone tiara that I'd bought at the costume store, because it made the purple streaks seem ironic.

Mrs. Baxter's gaze moved to my face. The majorette tryout guidelines had specified "full makeup" also. I was wearing an even heavier version of my usual smoky eye—maybe more of an evening look for most people rather than something they would wear during a dance tryout, but it went with my movie-star hair.

Her gaze shifted to my T-shirt. While the other girls

had opted for white or bright colors, mine had a picture of Courtney Love, for luck. If Courtney Love had tried out for majorette—which I was pretty sure she hadn't, because she was in juvie by the time she was my age—I thought she would have worn a tiara and striped her hair purple too. The new shirt was a lot smaller than what I usually wore, because I'd lost so much weight. But I was careful to make sure it wasn't too clingy. It disguised the stubborn roll of fat still hanging around my midriff. I wore long black shorts and thigh-high black-and-white-striped socks, because they amused me, and black Converse high-tops. This was the way I had dressed for my first two years of high school.

And I had fit in, more or less. I just wasn't someone you'd peg to try out for majorette. I'd gotten a lot of guff from my friends in band, especially Robert, for losing so much weight, trying out for majorette, and showing what a popular-girl wannabe I was. Trying out wearing my usual clothes with my usual purple hair was a concession I made to my friends, to show them I didn't think I was suddenly too good for them and their style. They were the only friends I had. Them and Addison. What a selection.

"Good luck," Mrs. Baxter said to me without emotion. I could tell that in her mind, I was not a contender. In my mind, I wasn't either. But I would try out. I would placate Addison and give Robert and the rest of the band something to talk about behind my back for the next few months. And after that, it would be over.

"Gemma Van Cleve," Ms. Zuccala called. I smiled my own brilliant smile and high-stepped into the gym, walking forward but facing sideways with my grin to the crowd, as Mrs. Baxter had taught us wannabes. There was a smattering of polite applause and an ugly groan from the band section. Before I could stop myself, I glanced in that direction and saw Robert, his dyed-black hair unnaturally glossy in the gymnasium lights, cupping his hands over his mouth to boo.

Reaching my designated place for the group routine, I turned forward, bent to place my third baton out of the way, and took my position with my arms extended, batons in hands. The booing had faded away with the applause. But the more I thought about it, the angrier I got, and the bigger I grinned. I would not make the majorette line, but I would twirl a flawless performance, and Robert could suck it.

Ms. Zuccala announced Addison, whose applause was a little louder than mine. Then came the girls behind her in line. They were a year older than us and had been majorettes this year. The applause for them was enthusiastic.

The school's fight song blared over the loudspeaker. It was a recording of the marching band. I was part of that marching band too. Only girls who'd been in band were allowed to try out. But for once, I wasn't playing alto sax. I was kicking and skipping in front of the band, pinwheeling my batons like a pro. If we'd been judged on our performance during the fight song alone, I would have been a shoo-in for majorette.

Some of the other girls had been taking baton for only a few months, since deciding to try out for majorette. Even Addison had dropped out of lessons in eighth grade—because baton was boring, or because I was a lot better than her, depending on whether you put more stock in what she said or how she acted. She'd started lessons again when she decided to try out. Only one of the juniors and I had been taking lessons for years. I even helped with the little kids' classes at the dance studio after school, just so I wouldn't have to go home.

I stayed on pattern, keeping my batons spinning in a plane, while the other girls' batons wobbled. I caught my tosses with the big end of the baton up to keep my spins neat, while the others grabbed their batons wherever they could. Not that the crowd would know the difference. What they *would* notice was how many times the other girls dropped their batons and had to chase them as they rolled away in a semicircle across the gym floor.

Sure enough, as the second stanza of the fight song began and all twenty of us wannabes attempted a high vertical toss while we turned underneath, three sickening thuds sounded, batons dropping to the wooden floor. Mine landed squarely in my hand. Another few thumb-flips, one toss caught behind our backs, and a horizontal twirl in one hand with a vertical twirl in the other just to make sure everybody was well coordinated, and we were done.

The recording stopped abruptly. The last strains of trombone echoed in the rafters. Two more batons thudded to the floor, and rubber soles squeaked on wood as girls scampered after them. I stood with both batons extended gracefully, my third baton on the floor next to my toe, right where it should be, and grinned my glamour smile. Really, the look was meant for Robert. I had *not* embarrassed myself as he'd told me I would. The applause was louder now.

Hot with exertion and adrenaline, I scooped up my extra baton and filed into the empty row of bleachers reserved for us. I sat between Delilah and Addison. Another sophomore strode to the middle of the floor and started her individual routine to a classical piano piece, of all things. I should have watched her. Instead, my mind spun with anger at the boys who had booed me. They were sitting directly behind me, six rows up.

Robert and I had been friends since the beginning of ninth grade. Addison and I sat next to each other in the alto sax section, but I couldn't shadow her *all* the time. I wanted to be an engineer someday, whereas she did anything she could to stay out of advanced math. That meant we didn't have every class together like we had in middle school. I'd fallen in with the art/drama/music geek crowd, where purple-streaked hair and Courtney Love T-shirts were the norm rather than the exception. And I'd fallen for Robert.

But he hadn't fallen for me. Everybody put up with the pudgy, quiet girl with the dry wit, but nobody *fell* for her. In ninth grade, Robert had hooked up with eighth graders too young to understand he wasn't as cool as he thought. Now that we were in tenth grade, he trolled for ninth graders. I had been the girl/friend he talked to about his girlfriends.

I should never have fantasized that he would finally fall in love with me when I lost weight. That was my own stupid fault. But he should not have made fun of me the way we'd both (I'll admit) made fun of the doll-like girls on other schools' majorette lines at football games last year.

Delilah's hand slipped into mine and squeezed, returning my thoughts to the competition, and the fact that eight girls had already taken their two-minute turns. Okay, I did not hold girls' hands. It smacked of sororities or beauty pageants or both. But I was not going to pull away from this panicking girl. I squeezed back.

Now Addison took my other hand. Without looking at her, I let her hold it. She'd never held my hand before, but she must have felt left out. I stared down at my hands, with Delilah's dark thighs on one side, Addison's white ones on the other. My own thighs were fifty percent larger than theirs.

I did not want to be here.

My insecurities were drowned out by Delilah's heavy breathing. "You're going to pass out," I whispered. "You need to calm down and breathe normally."

"Okay," she said between deep, abnormal breaths that were not helping at all.

I had to get her mind off her performance. I felt bad about talking through someone else's routine, but this was an emergency. I said the first thing that popped into my head. "Do you know Robert Cruise?"

She perked up immediately. "Cutie-pie!" she exclaimed. "With the hair, right?" She shook her hair out of her eyes in a terrific imitation of Robert. "Plays trumpet? He's in history with me. You're really good friends with him."

"I *thought* so," I said, "but he left me a sympathy card in my locker."

Her eyes got huge. "Like somebody *died*? Instead of a *good luck card*?"

She acted so horrified that I backtracked and defended him. "Yeah. It was supposed to be a joke. We send each other Grandparents Day cards on our birthdays and Halloween cards on Christmas and . . ."

I stopped because her brows went down in a scowl, and she was shaking her head sternly at me. "No. This is different. He does not send you a sympathy card on majorette tryout day. No."

That's what I'd thought when I saw the card. But I could hear Robert's excuse in my head, and I repeated it to Delilah. "Trying out for majorette is out of character for me. He never believed I wanted to do it. I guess the card was his last-ditch attempt to talk me out of something I'll regret later."

"I don't care *what* it was," she seethed loudly enough that Addison leaned forward to look at us curiously. "That is un-ac-ceptable!" She sounded just like her dad, whom I'd had for eighth-grade algebra. "This tryout is a big deal. It's taken a huge amount of work. You wouldn't be here if you didn't want to be a majorette."

"True," I said, because it *sounded* true, whether it was or not.

"Friends support each other no matter what," Delilah said firmly. "Oh God."

I looked up to see what she'd gasped at. The twirler in front of us was finishing her routine by chasing both her batons across the floor. Now it was Delilah's turn. Dropping Addison's hand, I hugged Delilah hard. Over the applause, I shouted, "You'll do great!" and meant it.

Delilah groaned. Her eyes flitted around like she was making sure she had space to faint on the floor.

I took her by the shoulders and looked into her eyes. "Don't think about all these people. Keep your eyes on me. I'll send you good thoughts."

"Okay." Delilah strutted onto the middle of the floor and grinned through the cheers and cat-calls, but sure enough, she watched me. I smiled at her.

"Traitor," Addison said in my ear.

"I can cheer for more than one friend," I said without looking at Addison.

"I mean, you didn't tell me about your third baton. You told me *not* to use a third baton. And all because *you* planned to steal my trick."

"I did not *steal* the concept of twirling a third baton from you," I said reasonably. "And I told you not to use a third baton because you would drop it." Which was true. But I had snuck my third baton in behind her back. I did not have to approve everything with Addison, but I *had* hidden this from her, which was not what a good friend would do.

She scooted away from me on the bench, toward the girl on the other side of her, putting as much space between us as she could—one symbolic centimeter.

I tried not to think about it. I watched Delilah. She

executed a perfect toss-up with a two-turn, then an illusion, kicking up one leg and twirling the baton beneath her, spinning her body as she went. I cheered for her, and whenever she glanced my way, I let her see in my face how great she was doing. I really liked Delilah—she was one of the few genuinely nice human beings I'd ever met—and I wanted her to do well. Also, focusing on her routine kept my mind off me. And Addison. And Robert.

Delilah struck a pose with her batons crossed above her head, signaling her finish. The gym exploded with applause. I jumped up, eager to make it to the center of the gym before I decided to run out the door instead.

"Break a leg," Addison said.

I turned. She scowled up at me without a hint of goodwill in her face. I was pretty sure she wasn't really wishing me good luck, and she wouldn't have minded if I'd broken a leg for real.

I high-stepped majorette-style to the center of the gym. Then I carefully placed my third baton to one side on the floor and put my hands holding the other batons on my hips. As I waited for my music to start, I stared at the back wall, feeling I did not have a genuine friend in this entire crowd of twelve hundred.

"Shake it, Gemma!" came a shout of five or six voices. The rest of the crowd giggled and looked to see who had yelled. They might not be able to tell, but I could. Robert and the trumpets around him bent their heads, hiding their faces.

If I'd had any lingering doubts about whether I should be furious with Robert, they were gone now.

My music started, thankfully. And for once in my life, I felt like I had total control. I'd picked a song with a booming disco beat that I knew the crowd would love. To keep their attention, I twirled one baton while I tossed the other incredibly high and turned three times beneath it. I had snuck into the gym and practiced to make sure my Converses wouldn't get hung up with too much traction on the slick floor. Before I could panic, the heavy baton smacked into my outstretched hand.

The crowd roared.

I concentrated on my routine, determined to make it through. I had choreographed the song with my body in mind. I did some toss-ups with double and triple turns, my flashy specialty. But my back was to the audience for only a split second each turn. Other than that, I never turned my back on the crowd. The trumpets had already told me to shake it, but nobody was going to shout "wide load" during *my* number.

I hadn't included any illusions, either, a staple of advanced routines. Delilah had impressed the crowd with one. She had a cute figure. But I refused to expose the insides of my thighs. This was why, though my baton teacher had told me I was her best student, I had never competed. I had never performed at all, except for the mandatory dance recitals at the end of the year. I kept my thighs to myself.

Carefully placing a second baton on the floor so it wouldn't roll away, I flipped the other on my elbows and spun it on the back of my neck. It wasn't hard once you got the hang of it, but it looked impressive. Only one junior with a lot of baton experience had this in her routine. The crowd noise now was an impressed "Oooooh."

I swept up my batons. It was time for my grand finale: juggling all three of them. This was a trick for a feature twirler, an expert who performed an independent routine on the football field. A regular majorette didn't need a move like this in her arsenal. Majorette routines for the halftime show were dumbed down to the lowest common denominator. If the whole line couldn't do a trick, none of the twirlers would do it.

But *I* would. As my song drew to a close, I gave the last baton some extra oomph, caught the one I already had in the air, spun around twice, and caught the last baton. I'd tossed it so high that it reached terminal velocity on the way down and clobbered my hand as it connected with my palm. I did not wince. I grinned until my cheeks ached, and I put my hands on my hips.

Then I prepared to transfer all three batons to one sweaty palm so I could use the other hand to shoot the whole gym the bird. Ms. Zuccala would surely suspend me. Addison wouldn't speak to me for a week because she would be embarrassed I was her friend. Robert and the music crowd would shun me because they would know the gesture was meant for them. But to tell them publicly how I felt about the way they'd treated me, it would be worth it.

Before I could shift my batons, the entire audience jumped up with a yell so loud, I felt the force of it in my chest.

Except for Addison, who was bent over in the bleachers, getting up her nerve. I was sorry she had to follow me. I could still shoot the gym the bird, removing myself from the competition. I had dropped a baton on purpose at our dance recital in sixth grade because Addison had dropped hers twice. I hadn't wanted her to hate me afterward for showing her up.

But removing myself from the contest out of fear of how my best friend would treat me, or out of spite—those were things I would do if I still thought I didn't have a chance of winning.

And now I thought I did.

I gripped my batons tightly and high-stepped back to the bleachers. I passed Addison as she marched on. She did not give me a high five.

A few hours later, at the end of the day, Ms. Zuccala came over the loudspeaker and called the majorette candidates into her office—probably so the Losers didn't swoon in public, fall into their Bunsen burners in chemistry lab, and sue the school for pain and suffering. Personally, I would have preferred to stay *en classe de français*. Nobody there had ever spoken to me except in French as directed by the teacher, asking me to bring them a *citron pressé*. But today at least five people leaned across the aisle to tell me I'd done a great job in tryouts. I enjoyed being the center of friendly attention for the first time in my life, and I dreaded what would happen next. Addison was in English then. I did not want to face her.

When I dragged myself into Ms. Zuccala's crowded office, Addison didn't rush over to me and hug me. She glanced at me out of the corner of her eye and deliberately turned her back, laughing with the popular juniors like she was working the room. Delilah talked with someone else. I didn't really know the other girls. Several of them looked at my hair—I was still wearing the tiara—then down at my shoes, and took one step backward. Since I was cornered by a huge glass trophy case, I pretended to be interested in the awards inside: the state football championship last year, the wrestling championship from a few years before, and lots and lots of trophies the majorette line had won at band contests.

"May I have your attention, please," Ms. Zuccala called. The giggling and shrieking quieted. Ms. Zuccala spoke to us and into the microphone, which broadcast across the school. We could hear her voice and her echo on the loudspeaker from the waiting room.

She consulted a slip of paper for several end-of-the-school-day announcements. Finally she winked at the room and said, "The moment we've all been waiting for. The members of the new majorette line are, in alphabetical order: Delilah Allen."

Everyone around Delilah smothered her in a group hug. Several girls squealed and shushed themselves, because whatever we said could be heard over the intercom. I imagined those squeals would be funny to hear if you were sitting in band. It was the sort of thing Robert and I would have rolled our eyes at together.

But I finally understood the emotion behind those squeals. I was thrilled for Delilah. When I'd heard her name, I'd let out the tiniest squeal myself. At least some good had come out of this warped experience. She'd wanted so badly to make the line. Now if she could figure out how not to faint on the football field during the halftime show next fall, she would be golden.

Ms. Zuccala called two juniors' names, and they jumped up and down together. Then, "Addison Johnson."

Addison put both hands to her mouth. That was all I saw before she was obscured by girls hugging her. I was happy she'd made the squad. Really happy. If I kept telling myself this, maybe I would feel it.

No . . . I was a terrible person, because all I felt was dread. She had made the majorette line, and I hadn't. She would lord it over me. She would hang out with the other majorettes from now on. I would go crawling back to Robert and admit that he'd been right. Majorette tryouts were a popularity contest. They had nothing to do with talent, since Addison had made it.

Ms. Zuccala called a junior's name. Addison walked over to Delilah, hugged her, and whispered to her. Addison very deliberately did not look at me. I should have approached them and hugged them both. But I knew Addison had not forgotten the three-baton fiasco. When she was in this mood, she would stare at me coldly and turn her back on me.

Luckily, the stress of the majorette announcements would be over in the next ten seconds. The girls whose names hadn't been called made fists and squeezed their eyes shut like they had a chance of making the squad, even though the alphabetical order had already passed them over. Didn't they realize this? The last girl called had been an *S*. There were only two people left in the room who could possibly make the squad: Charlene Tandekar and—

"Gemma Van Cleve," Ms. Zuccala announced.

I froze. Was she still calling out the names of the girls who'd made the line? Or had I been daydreaming, and she'd moved on to the names of the Losers?

Bodies jostled me from all sides. People were jumping up and down and hugging me, I realized after a few panicked seconds. I pasted my majorette grin on my face and hugged them back. I might even have managed a squeal. I was a majorette now. My brain told me I should be happy, but all I felt was numb.

Several of the girls who hadn't made it burst out of Ms. Zuccala's office to have a dramatic cry. The more gracious losers congratulated the new majorettes. Through the bustle, Addison snuck between girls and finally reached me. She threw her arms around me and hugged me hard enough to hurt. Then she whispered in my ear, "I'm so glad you made it. Now you can vote for me for head majorette." She held me at arm's length. "Our moms are going to be so happy! We're majorettes together, just like they were!"

"Yeah," I managed. Addison's mom would be ecstatic. I wasn't sure my mom really cared, but she would act politely cheerful. Maybe my dad would be happy for me. I would call him to tell him the news, but sometimes he didn't return my calls for a month, and he usually called back during school when he must know my ringer was off.

Addison was definitely happy. She would be voted head majorette for our senior year. The only other choices were Delilah, who was too nervous, and me.

I was not the type to be head majorette. I was not the type to be a majorette at all. Slowly my brain was processing what had happened to me. The school had chosen me for my talent, despite the purple streaks in my hair and my weight. I should be happy. Instead, I worried that being a majorette with Addison would provide her with new ways to torture me.

The final bell rang. I caught Delilah on her way out of Ms. Zuccala's office, overcame my natural disinclination to hugging, and gave her the big squeeze she deserved. As Addison and I jogged down the front stairs, into the bright spring afternoon, and walked down the hill to her car, all these kids I knew only vaguely or had never noticed before in my life waved to me as I passed and congratulated me. The third time this happened, Addison stomped her foot and protested, "I made majorette too!" I hoped for Addison's sake that they hadn't heard her.

My cell phone beeped with a text message. I only got texts from Addison, who was walking a few steps ahead of me, white fists squeezing the life out of her batons, and who obviously did not have her thumbs on her phone. And from Robert.

I stopped and dug out my phone. Robert had changed his mind, right? He was proud of me, and he'd convinced the rest of our band friends to be proud of me too. I clicked to his message.

You sold out.

There in the warm sunlight, I went cold, except for my cheeks, which felt like they were flaming hot.

Realizing I was not following her, Addison walked back to where I stood. She peered over my shoulder at the message.

"I guess he doesn't want to be friends anymore," I said, trying to sound like I didn't care.

"He's such an ass." Addison had always hated Robert. "If he *did* want to be your friend, you'd be insane to be his."

Addison was never right about anything. But I had to admit, at least silently to myself, that she'd hit on the truth this time. Robert knew I didn't want to be a majorette, but he also knew the tryout was important to me, if only for warped reasons. We'd been friends for two years. We'd sat together on every band trip when Addison was with her boyfriend of the week and Robert's younger girlfriend wasn't around. I had achieved something, and he owed me more than an insult.

Thinking about this, I realized that I *had* achieved something. Addison was looking over my shoulder, interested in *my* social life, rather than the other way around. That had never happened before. *Never*, in the six years we had been best friends. Now that I was a majorette (I was a majorette! So weird!), I might actually *get* a social life. Every majorette at my school had one—a real one that included boyfriends, not just unrequited crushes.

But I would need to fight for mine. For the first time ever, I was enjoying some mediocre level of social acceptance. Unless I took immediate action, I would lose my newly favorable position at my school when my fat roll was exposed to the world. Every week this fall, I would be forced to wear a skintight sequined leotard on a football field in front of the entire student body and thousands more people packing the stadium. I was determined not to be the comic relief.

I would have to lose more weight.

2

August

I saw him first, before Addison did. He was tall, slender, and Asian, and he kicked the football with the same purpose and economy of motion I tried for when I twirled batons. Every muscle in his body and every thought in his head focused on punting that ball perfectly across the football stadium. After his leg followed through with the powerful kick, he landed on the grass and watched the ball as it sailed through the goalposts, yet another score.

Then he turned around *again* and his dark eyes met mine *again*. The first time this had happened, I had assumed I was imagining things. Boys did not look at me. They saw through me. He must have been looking at some statuesque majorette behind me. When he huddled with his coach, I actually turned to see what he had been looking at on our end of the field. A hundred girls twirled thumb-flips in unison. I was on the end of the front row, and nobody stood directly behind me. He must have been looking at Addison beside me, then. But if he were, the tilt of his head would have been different, I thought. He really did seem to be looking at me.

Over and over.

This was the third and final day of majorette camp for Addison and me. The camp was taught by college majorettes and feature twirlers and was held on the campus of Georgia Tech. I'd had some idea that we might pass hot college guys walking back and forth between the gym and the caf. I would never have talked to them. I was not Addison. But I wanted to *look* like I could have talked to them. Keeping up my personal style was a challenge now that I'd lost almost fifty pounds in nine months. Even my Courtney Love T-shirt had gotten so big that it flowed around me like a muumuu. I could only wear it by safety-pinning a pleat into the back of it, which was getting uncomfortable.

I hadn't had a lot of time to go shopping, because I'd spent pretty much my whole summer teaching little girls at the dance studio, then rehearsing with the marching band. And honestly, new clothes hadn't been a big concern of mine until now. I never noticed my old clothes didn't fit anymore until I put them on and they fell off. I had no choice but to replace my shorts, because I couldn't be dropping my pants in public. But I didn't want to buy a lot of new tops yet. I had plenty of money from my allowance and working at the dance studio. I was just afraid that if I bought clothes, I would stay that size. I was not finished losing weight.

So the first day at camp, I wore one of my few shirts that fit. The second day, I wore the other. By day three I'd figured out that camp was held entirely in a gym set apart from campus foot traffic. All the cute college nerds had gone home for the summer anyway. Besides, I was out of clean laundry. I wore my MARCHING WILDCATS T-shirt, which fit because we'd turned in our sizes only a few weeks before.

Of course on *this* day, the instructors decided to move us to the huge football stadium for the afternoon so we could get a taste of what twirling would be like if we tried out for a college majorette line. And while high school majorette camp was going on at one end of the stadium, high school football camp was going on at the other.

But with this guy staring across the football field at me (I hoped), I was glad for once that I was not dressed with my usual edge. My MARCHING WILDCATS T-shirt could have passed for band geekdom or, wonder of wonders, school spirit. And in certain circles, the purple streaks in my hair, which I was wearing in two low ponytails down my back to combat the August heat, could have been misconstrued as fashionable.

Was he really *looking at me*? Nothing would come of it, of course. He wasn't from my high school. He could be from one of countless other high schools in Atlanta or from a tiny town hours away. I would never see him again after the camp session ended in a few minutes. In the meantime, it was nice to dream.

A group of twenty hulking quarterbacks passed footballs to one another. They threw balls down the field in a hailstorm of pigskin. They ran complicated formations that the coach halted every few seconds, before they could fully execute them, which must have been frustrating.

My guy was in a different group. Each player had a tall, slender kicker's body. The coach of this group talked more. He explained with his hands, and from the looks of it, whatever he was telling them involved astrophysics. Each time his lecture ended, the boys would line up to kick the ball through the goalposts. Whether I was doing thumbflips or one-turns, I made sure I watched my guy, from his step up to the tee to the follow-through of his kick.

His legs were long and muscular. His shirt stuck to his chest with sweat. His longish hair bounced as he ran up to the ball and punted it. The coach would talk to him after each turn, pointing down the field. But from my lay-chick's point of view, this boy did not need camp. He put the ball through the uprights every time.

And then he turned around to see if I was watching. I couldn't tell at that distance whether he was hot. But his stare showed that he unabashedly appreciated the movements of girls—or, just possibly, *this* girl. That was hot.

The football camp ended with one last pep talk. The kickers gathered around their coach, and the quarterbacks gathered around theirs. Occasionally the coaches' voices rang so loudly against the stadium seats that I could hear them over my own instructor counting thumb-flips. Soon the kickers shouted "Break!" and moseyed off the field.

But not my guy. He stood on the sideline and watched the quarterbacks like he was waiting for one of them. Finally the quarterbacks shouted "Break!" and a towering blond guy headed for my guy. I knew the blond was huge because my guy had seemed tall before, half a head above his coach, but the blond was another half a head above him, and almost twice as wide. They stood together by the exit that the other players had taken out of the stadium. My guy said something to the blond. They both turned and looked at me.

My heart sped up, even faster than it had each time my guy had caught my eye.

While they talked, they nonchalantly crossed their arms

and pulled up the sides of their shirts to reveal hard six-pack abs like nothing I had ever seen in real life, possibly because I still, out of habit, avoided the community pool.

As if in slow motion, they exposed their muscular chests.

Triceps flexing, they pulled the shirts over their heads.

They stood there, chatting, wiping their faces and chests with the cloth. Admittedly, I had never played sports, and I did not hang out where the athletic boys hung out, so maybe I was misreading the entire situation. But it sure looked to me like the high school football player's striptease. I enjoyed it way more than I meant to. I started to feel like a stereotypical guy gawking at girls and accidentally running his car into a pond.

They both pulled clean T-shirts from the mesh bags at their feet and shrugged them on. But they hung around. And I could have sworn that every few seconds, my guy still glanced over at me.

"Check out those hotties," Addison said to me out of the corner of her mouth. I stole a look at her between thumb-flips. She nodded toward the guys. "When this slave driver finally lets us out of camp, *run* with me over to those boys, so we can stake our claim before the rest of these desperate females."

Hanging out with Addison was always dramatic. I considered myself to be an intelligent, reasonable person who had seen more than my share of teen girl hysteria, because of her.

"Normally, if I saw strangers staring at me, I *would* run right over and introduce myself," I said. "But I'm not convinced they're staring at me. They could be watching any of these girls."

"They're *not* staring at you," Addison said. "They're staring at *me*." Her thumb-flips grew larger like she was trying to get the boys' attention. I moved away from her so I wouldn't get hit. On my other side, some football equipment on the sidelines was in my airspace—a sled with man-shaped pads that linebackers pushed down the field. I edged back toward Addison.

"If these boys want to stare at me," she went on, "I'm there." On *there* she spun an extra-hard thumb-flip—so hard that it flew straight at me and dinged me on the nose. The blond guy pointed and laughed. My guy took a step forward, almost as if the baton strike were life-threatening and he was going to run to my aid.

The tip of the baton was made of rubber, so it didn't hurt too much at first. But in the next split second, the shock hit me. I dropped my baton, covered my nose with both hands, and *aargh*ed at the pain.

I used to have the cutest little nose. Then, one day when I was eleven, I was driving a go-cart around my mom's yard with Addison in the passenger seat. Addison decided it was her turn to drive, jerked the steering wheel out of my hands, and ran us into a tree. The steering wheel broke my nose. When the swelling went down, I had a bump. My mom offered to get me plastic surgery this summer to fix it—"You will look so much better, and feel better about yourself, you'll see"—but no way was I going under a knife just for looks.

At least, that's what I'd thought until I pictured what I must look like with a new red bump from Addison's baton on top of my already prominent schnoz. There went any chance I'd had of capitalizing on my guy's interest in me.

I tried to resign myself to this and concentrate on making the pain go away. Ever since Addison had broken my nose, when I got hit there, it was like getting hit on my funny bone, a deep inescapable pain so bad it almost tickled. Pesky anger at her remained. But she didn't *always* mess things up for me and boys, did she? No, because I had never had any "things" with boys before. She only had a habit of embarrassing me in front of guys who mattered to me, whether I mattered to them or not.

"All right, ladies!" the instructor called. The other girls stopped twirling and gathered around her to hear her last few tidbits of wisdom while I stood behind them, clutching my nose, wishing the pain would suddenly clear so I could smile over at the boys like it was no harm, no foul. The pain would not relent.

There was a rush around me as we were released from camp. "Here," Addison said, pulling one of my hands free from my nose and thrusting something into it, which felt like my baton bag with all three batons inside. Then I was being dragged across the grass by my elbow, which of course was attached to my arm, attached to my hand, pressed desperately to my throbbing nose. She was dragging me over to those boys *anyway*.

"Really?" I asked. My voice came out extra nasally.

"Really," Addison said. "And if you can't say anything non-snarky, please say nothing at all." We reached the sideline, and she let go of my elbow. "I saw you staring," she told the boys. "You boys like what you see?"

"She is completely serious," I explained to them with my hand still to my nose.

Both boys laughed. My guy asked me, "Are you okay?"

He was tall and paler than most of the football players we'd seen who'd been frying in the sun all summer. His deep black hair had resisted any reddish sun streaks and fell into his eyes. A perfect combination of sinewy body and delicate features, he looked like the lead singer for a Japanese pop band. Everybody at my school thought these bands were cool and had posters of them in their lockers, though nobody actually listened to their music because hello, their lyrics were in Japanese. In short, I had wondered from a distance whether this boy was hot, and he was.

I had given up on attracting him, though. Now it was only a matter of waiting until Addison was through throwing herself at these boys so we could go home. I would have preferred to make my way home on the MARTA subway by myself, clutching what was left of my face and my dignity. But Addison's mom would be horrified, and I would get in trouble with my mom if I left Addison to fend for herself in downtown Atlanta, even though Addison was six months older than me and had never missed a chance to remind me of this and boss me around when we were younger.

"I'll be okay in a minute," I mumbled. Still squinting against the pain, I released my nose, felt around for the metal bench that I'd noticed earlier, and sat down. I waved at them dismissively. "Y'all don't mind me. Flirt away."

Addison grilled the guys. "Who were you really watching?"

My guy laughed as the blond one exclaimed, "You!" He was cute too, but big enough to look dangerous. He stood with his muscular arms crossed like he was uncomfortable, protecting his tender feelings.

"Out of all those girls?" Addison asked, tilting her head so that her long blond hair curved down around her boob on one side, and—oh my God, was she pointing both toes in like a two-year-old? Yes, she was. "You're just saying you were watching me because I'm the one who came over here." The first intelligent words she'd uttered.

"Nooooo," said my guy. "We were watching you and your friend here. We were fascinated by that flippy thing you do with your baton."

"This?" Addison asked.

I deduced from the whirring noise that she was demonstrating her skills for them again. For safety, I slid farther away from her on the bench, then gingerly touched my nose. It would stay on. I dabbed my fingertips under my eyes to make sure my mascara hadn't run when I teared up. I wasn't wearing foundation because I would just sweat it off in the summer heat, but I was wearing heavy eye makeup, as always, to go with the purple streaks in my hair. If you were going to have purple hair, it didn't seem right to dress down.

"We're taking the MARTA home," Addison chirped, "but we're stopping by the Varsity for dinner first."

This was not strictly true. Addison had said we should stop there for dinner. I had told her no. The Varsity served killer burgers and dogs and fries. It was exactly the kind of place I tried to stay away from now that I was losing weight.

"Y'all want to come with us?" she asked.

"Addison," I said sternly. "They could be serial killers."

"That's a separate camp," said my guy.

"*We* could be the serial killers," Addison protested. "Are you boys scared we'll attack you if you walk to the Varsity with us? Chicken? Bock-bock-bock!" She led the way out of the stadium, with the guy formerly known as *my guy* beside her.

Shaking my head to clear it of the pain, I used my baton as a walking stick and hoisted myself up from the bench. With nothing else to do but trail along like lost puppies, the quarterback and I fell in behind Addison and my kicker. Awk. Ward!

So it was clear from the beginning that Addison and my guy, her chosen one, were bonding. The odd man out and I, who had no interest in each other, were waiting around for them until they finished.

I should have been thrilled that we were hanging with these boys who didn't know I'd been fifty pounds heavier last November. Their names were Clean and Slate. But if I'd thought my only problem was being overweight, that idea faded as I tried to come up with something to say to this blond demigod. All the stars were aligned and I *still* couldn't make small talk. Meanwhile, Addison walked ahead of us, chatting away with my guy.

In these situations I found it best to call up a surge of

adrenaline and pretend to be extroverted. I'm not saying it *was* best. My extroverted imitation tended to get out of hand sometimes. I'm just saying I *found* it best. I switched my baton bag to my left hand and stuck out my right hand. "I'm Gemma Van Cleve, by the way."

"I'm Carter Nelson." The blond took my hand and moved it up and down gently, like he was afraid of breaking it. Which was good, because his huge, meaty paw could have wrapped around my hand twice if he were exceedingly limber and human anatomy worked that way.

"And that's Max Hirayama." He nodded toward my guy and Addison as we emerged onto the tree-lined sidewalk.

Addison looked around like she was disoriented until Max pointed to the left. "This way," he said.

"Wow, how do you know your way around so well?" Addison asked in the you-are-so-big-and-strong voice she used when flirting with boys or getting pulled over for speeding by policemen.

"My dad is a professor here," Max said.

"Your dad is a professor at Georgia Tech?" Addison shrieked. "You must be so smart! You must think we're so stupid!"

I wanted to suggest that she stop tossing that *we* around so loosely. But the two of them had headed up the sidewalk, leaving Carter and me behind.

Then I remembered that I was pretending to be a person who actually wanted to talk to other people. "And that's Addison Johnson," I told Carter. "Where are y'all from?"

He named a high school just southeast of ours. They were one of our biggest rivals in academics, band, and sports, but especially football. "Oh, we play you our first game!" I burst out. "We're going to kick your ass."

I was kidding, of course. Both teams were great, and the outcome of the game was always a toss-up. Carter should have understood and responded with a grin and a snappy comeback.

But Max overheard me, stopped, and turned to stare at me wide-eyed in horror as Carter moaned, "Ooooooh, don't say that where Max can hear you. He's a kicker, and kickers are superstitious."

Addison turned too and narrowed her eyes at me, angry that I was sabotaging her chance with Max. As my body went into fight-or-flight mode, everything seemed to intensify: the glare of the early evening sun, the heat radiating from the sidewalk, the smell of asphalt, the swish of cars down the university road, and the softer roar of cars on the interstates tangled around the skyscrapers nearby. I *hated* when Addison got mad at me and gave me the cold shoulder until she needed something from me. Most of the time I hadn't meant to offend her, and there was nothing I could have done to prevent it. This time I honestly didn't understand what was so awful about what I'd said.

I cleared my throat and timidly tried to repair the damage. "Superstitious, how?"

"Max has never missed a kick in a game," Carter said.

"Wooowwwww," Addison said, even though she probably didn't even know what a record like that meant. I did, and I understood how impressive it was.

Carter shrugged. "He didn't start last year, so he didn't get that many chances."

"I made the kick every chance I had," Max defended himself.

"And when he made the first one," Carter said, "Max decided that everything has to go exactly the same way before games, or his mojo will disappear. It's ridiculous. He wears the same underwear every time."

Now Max was eyeing Carter with a look that said, *Shut up, Carter*. I knew how Max felt.

To lighten the mood, I asked Max, "Do you *wash* this underwear?"

"I do," he confirmed, but not in his jovial tone. He started walking toward the Varsity again. We all followed.

"Everything's already breaking routine," Carter went on. "Our first game won't be like the games last year. He met a beautiful girl from our rival team at football camp.

And then she tells him he's going to get his ass kicked? You've just caused Max a lot of sleepless nights."

"Gemma!" Addison reprimanded me, sliding her hand around Max's forearm.

Rather than being angry with Addison for being angry with me, now *both* of us were mad at me. I had ruined adorable Max's chance at a perfect season. He would probably get addicted to crack next, and it would be all my fault.

3

I hung back and let Max and Addison and Carter talk, removing myself from the conversation so I wouldn't attempt any more tricks that I wasn't skilled enough to handle, such as friendliness, or wit. We reached the bridge over sixteen lanes of interstate traffic. To our right was my favorite view of Atlanta, with the cars whizzing below us, grassy spaces bursting with pink flowers, and skyscrapers towering above it all, their glass panels reflecting the blue sky. I pretended to concentrate on the view—no, I wasn't pretending, I really *was* concentrating on it, or trying to—because I could think of nothing to say to this Carter person I'd been saddled with.

We all walked into the Varsity together but got divided at the vast counter when we placed our orders. Ten cashiers boomed, "WHAT'LL YA HAVE?" with no patience for socially handicapped teenagers. They insisted that we move the line along by splitting up instead of standing behind one another.

It was terrible of me, but I felt a brief moment of joy seeing that Max did not offer to pay for Addison's dinner. This didn't mean he *wasn't* into her, but he definitely presented no certification that he *was*.

I was the last person to get served, and none of the others waited for me before sitting down. The restaurant was huge, with lots of different rooms of seating. But predictably, Max and the others were all the way in the back, in an elevated room with a view of the skyline out one wall of windows, the Georgia Tech stadium out the second, and more skyline and the 1996 Olympics torch out the third. By the time I found them, Max was on one side of the booth with Addison next to him, and Carter was on the other side. I slid into the empty space.

As I sat down, I swear Addison glanced up at me, then scooted closer to Max as if to say, *Mine.* Like I hadn't gotten that message already.

"So, are you dating anybody?" she asked Max.

I cringed on her behalf. Addison had always told me

there was nothing wrong with flirting, and whenever I'd advised her to tone it down, she acted like she had no idea what I was talking about. She thought she was asking a casual question, "Are you dating anybody?" when she was actually yelling at Max, "DATE ME, DATE ME, DATE ME." At least she would run him off, talking like this. I wouldn't land him, but she wouldn't either.

Incredibly, Max did not ease out of the booth and run for his life. He smiled, and bright spots of color appeared on his cheeks. He said, "No, I'm not dating anyone right now."

"He makes girls mad," Carter laughed.

Max gave Carter another warning look, then gave up and chuckled along with him.

Addison gasped at Max. "You?"

I could only imagine what Carter meant, if both boys found it so funny. Maybe Max was known as a heartbreaker around his school. I could understand that. He was so handsome, with the edges of his eyes crinkling as he smiled.

Registering Carter's voice and remembering that he was sitting at the table too, Addison turned to him. "What about you?" she asked as an afterthought. "Dating anybody?"

"We just broke up," Carter said.

"Awwwwww," Addison said, poking out her bottom lip and giving him her sad, sad face.

Carter laughed again, though seemingly not out of embarrassment for her. He acted like he really enjoyed Addison's baby face. Boys were disgusting. I attacked my dinner.

Addison refocused her attention on Max. She teased him with inane comments I didn't bother to listen to. Max had a nice laugh that lit up his face, like he wasn't afraid to show his appreciation for a joke somebody else had made, unlike Robert, who only laughed at his own. Carter munched french fries.

In the midst of Addison's flirting, Max glanced up at me several times, his eyes so dark that they took me aback. At first I thought he was shooting me looks for ruining his kicking mojo. But he seemed so sympathetic that I started to wonder whether he was worried about me. I supposed I *had* gone silent very suddenly. There was a difference between keeping my mouth shut and sulking. So I sat up a little straighter and made a point to laugh periodically and interject a comment for every twenty of Addison's.

Suddenly she frowned at my plate and sneered, "What are you *eating*?"

"A grilled chicken sandwich," I said evenly. I'd been expecting this. The sandwich was good, but it wasn't what people normally ordered at the Varsity. She stuffed her face with a burger and fries. Carter chowed down on two of each. And Max—

—was eating a grilled chicken sandwich, I saw as I glanced over. Ha! With great restraint, I gazed deliberately at her, then nodded toward Max's tray like I was trying to stop her from offending him.

Her eyes slid to his sandwich and widened. She said without missing a beat, "Well, Max can probably eat whatever he wants to, Gemma. *You're* eating grilled chicken because you just lost fifty pounds."

Both boys stared at me, Carter stopping with a french fry halfway into his mouth.

I could feel myself turning bright red, but I just smiled sweetly at all of them.

"You *did*?" Carter finally asked.

"Yep." I took a bite.

"That is hard to picture," Max said.

Well, don't, I almost blurted, but it was too late. They already had.

"Don't you want some of my fries, Gemma?" Addison pointed to her plate. "Or the rest of my milkshake? Gosh, I can't finish it all, but I'll bet *you* could."

Have I mentioned that I did not like my best friend very much? After a sip of diet soda, I tried to pretend I wasn't mortified. I changed the subject by asking the boys, "What did y'all do at football camp?"

They looked at each other. Then Max said, "We were

actually in two different camps. We were divided up by position. So Carter was in quarterback camp—"

"You're the quarterback for your team?" Addison asked, genuinely interested in Carter for the first time. The quarterback for our own team was the most popular guy in school—so popular that even Addison, with her formidable powers of acting like a ditz so boys would like her, could not turn his head in her direction.

"Yeah," Carter said. A blush crept into his cheeks, and one corner of his mouth turned up in a tightly controlled grin. Aw, the big guy was embarrassed at the attention.

"There's more to you than meets the eye," Addison said in the same flirtatious tone she'd used with Max thirty seconds before. "You're silent but violent."

The boys and I burst into laughter. For the first time, I felt like *we* were sharing something and *she* was the odd chick out.

"What's so funny?" she asked.

I turned to Max to let him explain, but his lips were pressed together, suppressing a smile. I put Addison out of her misery. "That's a term usually reserved for describing a fart."

"Oh!" Sixteen emotions passed across her face in the space of half a second. Like magic, she turned the situation around. She leaned diagonally across the table and patted

Carter's muscular forearm, her bottom lip poked out in sympathy. "I didn't mean to call you a fart."

Carter's blue eyes widened. I thought he would be speechless. But then he said, "Max is the one who's full of hot air."

Incredible. Carter and Max were arguing over Addison. The table practically vibrated with their lusty thoughts for her.

I wasn't going to take that through the rest of my chicken sandwich. To return to a more comfortable subject, I asked Max, "So you were at, what? Kicker camp?" I could have sworn he'd been staring at me on the field—*me*, not Addison. If he had been, he would have seen me staring right back at him. Since that obviously was *not* what had been going on, I couldn't admit that I'd been watching him at practice and I'd seen what he'd done at kicker camp with my own eyes.

He did give me kind of a funny look, like he'd thought our eyes *had* met on the field and now he was confused. But he simply said, "Yeah. I'm not big enough to play any position but kicker. The first time I got tackled, I'd get squashed like a leetle bug."

He was making a joke before Carter could beat him to it, I thought. Max must be used to getting teased by his team about his size. But he was taller than average and not skinny, just lean. That had become clear to me when he took his shirt off. Every other guy on their team must look like Carter the oafburger.

"As rarely as he's on the field, he might as well not be on the team," Carter said.

Max's eyes slid to Carter, but his smile never changed. He took a breath to defend himself. For some reason, I felt compelled to do it for him.

"He might as well not be on the team?" I repeated. "Carter, how can you say that? There's a lot of pressure on the quarterback because you have so much to coordinate. But there's probably even more pressure on the kicker. Max is solely responsible for scoring a field goal or an extra point, and often that's the deciding score in a game."

Max turned to Carter. "What she said."

"But it doesn't really matter yet," I said, "unless you're starting seniors."

"We're both juniors," Max told me, "but we're both starting."

"You *are*?" I asked. "For *your* school? Wow, that's huge. You must both be really good."

Carter smiled and blushed, but Max gave me a savvier smile. "How do you know so much about football?" he asked. "You don't strike me as a girl who would watch football. You look like you'd be a fan of . . . I don't know." He tilted his head as he ran his eyes over my brown hair streaked with purple, down my MARCHING WILDCATS T-shirt, to my funky bracelet collection on my left arm—which I never went without, but which Addison complained was annoying to listen to when I twirled. He said, "Fight club."

Fight club wasn't quite the look I was going for. *Roller derby* would have been better. I didn't want Max to think I was harsh.

Over Carter's and Addison's chuckles, I said, "May I remind you that I am also a majorette for my high school marching band? That's me, Gemma Van Cleve, Incorporated, defying stereotypes for almost sixteen years."

"As a Japanese-American football player with a southern accent, I *might* know where you're coming from." Max winked.

"Touché." I grinned at him.

He grinned back at me, and the smile seemed genuine, reaching his deep brown eyes. I had never been good at flirting. When I was heavier, I'd had no confidence that boys would be interested in me, so I didn't bother trying. Even now that I'd lost weight and gained self-esteem, flirting was foreign. There was a fine line between sexy banter and out-and-out arguing. I tended to cross it and chase boys off. Or maybe I chased them off with my noisy bracelets. But in that moment, with Max, I felt like I had hit the elusive sweet spot. For once, I had done everything exactly right.

"What did you say?" Addison asked. "Tissue? Tush? What?" She wasn't really that stupid, I hoped. It must have been the only way she could think of to re-enter the conversation. While I'd held the boys' attention, she'd stripped the wrappers off three straws and braided them together. She did not do well when she wasn't the focus of attention.

"You have been left behind," I told her.

That was the wrong thing to say. Addison smiled at me humorlessly, face tight. I had lots of experience being dragged along on her flirting runs, but no experience getting caught up in one. She seemed to be telling me to get back into my cage and wait until she called me.

"I'll tell you how Gemma knows so much about football," Addison said.

Oh, she wouldn't. She'd already spilled to these boys that I'd lost almost a third of my body weight. Surely she wouldn't tell them about my dad, too?

Yep, she would. "When Gemma was little, she went to every Falcons game with her dad."

"Wow, every game?" Max asked. "That must have been expensive. He had season tickets?"

I swallowed. "Sort of."

Addison, seeing that this line of conversation caused me discomfort, generously made things worse. "Her dad owned the team."

Both guys gaped at me. Their eyes and mouths opened wide. They looked like cartoon characters with their jaws and eyeballs lolling on the floor. Boys were terrified by the idea of my rich and powerful dad, even though he was nowhere around and didn't care about me.

"He *used* to own the team," I clarified sheepishly. "Only part of the team. It was just an investment he held for a while." As the words came out, I knew I was digging a deeper hole for myself, lamely trying to explain away my dad's casual investment of several million dollars, but I couldn't stop. "He sold it when he moved to Hilton Head." Good work, Gemma! I had successfully downplayed how filthy rich my dad was by revealing that he lived in the most exclusive oceanside retreat for Atlanta executives.

My face burned so hot that my whole body started to sweat in the air-conditioned restaurant. I managed to mumble, "I forgot I need to text my mom," as I jumped up from the table and hurried in the direction of the restaurant exit. Too late, I realized that was also the direction of the restrooms. The boys probably thought I had bladder control issues.

In front of the long row of cash registers, a display case held photos of the Varsity in the 1950s and 1960s and signed pictures of stars who'd eaten there or used to work there. I parked myself at the picture of Ryan Seacrest, maybe from back when he was a deejay in Atlanta, looking very 1990s with his hair spiked and frosted.

I'd only wanted to escape the boys' scrutiny for a moment. But as I leaned against the wall, I really did text my mom. She was picking me up at the MARTA stop, and this whole side trip of Addison's would put me home an hour later than I'd told her. As I thumbed *L-a-t-e*, Addison rushed toward me in a cloud of blond, her blue eyes huge, lips pursed and barely hiding a smile, fists balled in excitement. "Guess what!"

Uh-oh. "What?"

"Max asked me out! He works as a soccer referee on Saturdays and Sundays, and their school starts back Monday like ours, but he wants to go out with me next Friday night!"

"That's great!" I forced out as my heart sank into my gut. *Oh no.* I had liked Max so much—way more than any boy I'd ever known for only an hour—and though Addison had been flirting hard with him, I'd begun to hope he would see that *I* was the girl for him. He was fascinating and quirky. He belonged with the quirky sidekick friend, *not* the popular princess friend. What was he thinking? *How could he?*

But as I stared at Addison in shock, I took in her asymmetrical shirt and crazy, colorful, dangling earrings, which I'd convinced her to buy on clearance so she'd have something in her closet besides preppie pastels. Max didn't know this.

Maybe he'd mistaken *Addison* for the quirky sidekick friend. That was the only explanation. And my purple hair and bracelet collection really *had* passed for fashion. I had sat there paralyzed and mostly speechless while Addison had flirted with Max and told him how rich my dad was. He had thought I was snobby, not socially awkward. I had changed the way my body looked, but I couldn't change the way I acted. In a battle with Addison over a boy, Addison would always win. I had never intended this or imagined it would happen in my lifetime, but I had been mistaken for the popular friend, and the boy I'd been looking for thought I was not his type.

Damn it!

Addison grinned her toothy majorette grin at me. "And you're going out with Carter!"

4

"I'm going out with Carter? The quarterback?" I acted confused, but really I was fishing for information. I hoped she'd gotten the two boys mixed up. Addison had a date with Carter, and I had a date with Max. This scenario was unlikely but not beyond the realm of possibility. After all, she *had* flirted with Carter, too. She had rubbed Carter's arm and told him he was not a fart. Maybe he'd gotten the message and asked to go out with her.

Wrong. "*Yes*, you're going out with Carter the quarterback!" she said. "You two are so cute together."

I found this highly doubtful. To figure out what had

actually happened, I played along. "And I can tell you really like Max."

"He is *so hot*," she confirmed.

No argument there. But he was more than just hot to me. He was hot *and* hilarious, the perfect guy. Carter was not. Luckily, I didn't have to worry about that. "See, here's the thing, Addison," I said slowly enough for her to understand. "Carter didn't ask me out." In fact, if I never saw or heard from Carter again, I wouldn't have been surprised. She could go out with Max once, and I would try to forget the whole funny conversation with him had ever happened.

"Yes, Carter *did* ask you out." Addison nodded, as if that would be enough to convince me.

"He did? Where was I when this happened, and what did I say?"

She rolled her eyes. "I mean, we're all four going out together."

I ran my hand back through my hair. Or tried, but my fingers got caught in the back-combing I'd used to make my ponytails look more rock-and-roll. I put my hand down with a frustrated sigh. "Who says we're all four going out together?"

"*I* say. My mother would never let me go out with a boy without having you there. Especially when she didn't grow up with his parents."

Addison was, in general, full of shit. But she was not making this up. Bad things had happened in her family. Her mom had divorced her dad, with good reason, and now her mom kept a tight rein on the four kids. I would have guessed that's what had pushed Addison into becoming the biggest flirt in school, except she had been like that already.

The one way Addison could go anywhere she wanted was if she took me along. It was a running joke between us. She would ask her mom if she could go to a concert. Her mom would say no before the words got out of Addison's mouth. Then Addison would add that I was going. Addison's mom would tell her to have a good time and ask her if she needed any money. We had plans to test how far we could push this by having Addison tell her mom we were going to visit her boyfriend in prison, but we hadn't gotten around to it yet.

The thing was, Addison's mom wanted Addison to hang out with me because I was rich, and my mom was in charge of the elite circles of Atlanta society that Addison's mom wanted so badly to join. My mom didn't mind me hanging out with Addison because her mom was always willing to invite me over, which got me out of my mom's way. Addison and I had become best friends in fifth grade without any say in the matter at all.

"Addison," I said, "Max wants to go out with you, but

Carter doesn't want to go out with me. I'm not dating Carter just because you say so."

"Max says so too. He says the Dolly Paranoids are playing in a concert hall at Little Five Points, and he can drive us all down there."

"What! You're kidding!"

She raised her eyebrows at me. "You've heard of the Dolly Paranoids?"

"Yes, they're awesome!" Now I was excited about this date—even if it *was* with Carter. "Album 88 plays them a lot." Addison was so square, she probably hadn't heard of the indie rock radio station at Georgia State, either. "The Dolly Paranoids are sort of a country speed-metal band."

"Max thinks they're awesome too," she said doubtfully. "Carter didn't seem too thrilled."

I couldn't picture Carter being thrilled about *anything*.

"We've already decided Carter will pick me up because he lives closer to me," she said, "and Max will pick you up because he lives closer to you. We'll meet in the middle and drive down together. It's a done deal."

Wait a minute—Max was picking me up instead of Carter? I'd have to make small talk with the guy who'd chosen Addison over me? I was not excited about the date anymore. "It can't be a done deal when you didn't even tell me about it!"

"I'm telling you now." She paused. "You don't like Carter?"

"Sure, I like him fine," I lied.

"Then why won't you go out with us?" she whined. "Are you afraid you'll say something dumb in front of Max again?"

I felt my cheeks turn hot, which made me angry at myself. Now Addison would think she'd guessed right, when she hadn't. I was reluctant to go, but not because I would embarrass myself. I wasn't even feeling very jealous. I'd liked Max a lot, but the fact that he'd asked Addison out lowered my opinion of him. Which didn't say a whole lot for my friendship with Addison, but there it was.

No, I didn't want to go because I was tired of being Addison's chaperone. She was a teenager having all the fun, and I was a million years old.

"Please, Gemma." Addison poked out her bottom lip.

Had she said . . . *please*? To *me*? She must have been delirious from the milkshake sugar rush.

"This will be my first chance to go on an actual date," she said.

Right. It was always about her. I wasn't doing it this time. Not anymore. I opened my mouth to protest.

She saw she was losing me and added quickly, "*Your* first chance too. Your first date ever will be with a gorgeous blond hunk who's the quarterback of the rival football team! What do you think Robert and the rest of the trumpets will say to *that*?"

Robert and the rest of the trumpets would make some very funny, very lewd jokes about it. And if meaty Carter found out what they'd said about me and showed up at school to defend me, they would run hide in the girls' bathroom. What sweet revenge for the way Robert had treated me!

"Okay," I said. "Sure. I'll go out with Carter." I felt like I was jumping off the high dive as I said it. Granted, I hadn't been off the high dive since I was little, but I remembered that feeling: a burst of carefree energy, a sense of complete freedom, followed by an ache in the pit of my stomach as I looked down and realized what I'd done.

"Great! I'll go tell the guys." She flounced away without bothering to say *Thank you, Gemma*, or *I owe you one, Gemma*, or *Next time we both like the same boy, you can have him, Gemma*.

Grumbling to myself, I finished my text message to my mom and hit send.

With heavy feet, I dragged myself back to the table. Hoping they'd finished eating so we wouldn't have to carry on our awkward conversation any longer—at least not for another week, hooray!—I stood next to Carter. If anybody expected me to throw myself in his lap, they were going to be disappointed.

Nope, nobody seemed to expect this. Neither Carter nor Max looked up at me. Addison chatted away animatedly even though nobody seemed to be paying attention. When she saw me, she said, "Speak of the devil!"

Oh God. I did not even want to know what she meant by that. I smiled glamorously. The majorette grin was coming in handy lately for both of us.

"Ready to go?" Max smiled, too, as he asked this, but he sounded about half as happy as he had before I left the table. Depressed that he'd made a date with Addison, probably. Served him right.

"Yes!" Addison and I said in unison. Addison was enthusiastic. I was faking it like the Best Majorette Ever. She gave me a playful little slap on the face for saying the same thing she'd said at the same time. Her reaction would have been kind of cute if I had not been about to strangle her.

Thankfully, it was another short walk from the Varsity to the MARTA station. The sidewalk was crowded with rush hour pedestrians—Georgia Tech students with backpacks and businesspeople who worked in the skyscrapers. Small talk was impossible while we were surrounded. As we descended the stairs into the station, a train was waiting. I thought we would catch it and be spared more small talk, but noooo! Just as we reached the platform, the doors closed and the train pulled away.

Dejectedly, I sat down on a concrete bench set into a wall covered in a bright tile mural. Max and Addison talked as they walked toward me. Carter lagged behind. If models in men's fashion magazines were supposed to look buff and sullen, he had a job waiting for him in case this quarterback thing didn't work out.

To my surprise, Max sat beside me on the bench. Addison sat beside him. Even though there was space on my other side, Carter sat beside her.

Well, of course. Carter didn't want to go out with me. Both Carter and Max wanted to go out with Addison. Max had been hooked from the first flirt, and now Carter had gotten on board. I often felt like the odd chick out when Addison tried to land a guy, but this time I wasn't even the third wheel. I was the fourth wheel. On our "date," I would end up watching as both guys fought over her, like they were contestants on one of those dating shows, and I was someone hired to clean the set.

"You don't seem happy," Max whispered.

I turned to find him unexpectedly close. Staring into his dark eyes, I didn't realize for a full five seconds that he'd been whispering to *me*.

I couldn't admit I'd been pouting that Addison always got the guy. Or guys. So I nodded toward the tile mural behind us, which depicted pastureland in primary colors with billowing clouds in the blue sky. "I was puzzling over the ironic decor."

He laughed. "I can just see the caption on the public service announcement: 'See this beautiful scene? We razed the field to give you this MARTA station.'"

I played along. "'And see how we have improved the bucolic landscape with clouds of smog?'"

Now that I was enjoying the small talk, of course a train screeched into the station. It was full enough at rush hour that we all got separated for a moment, with Addison grabbing the only empty seat and the rest of us hanging on to the poles. I gripped my baton bag, made myself as small as possible in the crowd, and tried not to lose my balance while both boys and fifty onlookers could see.

Several stops later, as the train slid into Carter and Addison's station, Addison jumped up. She gave Max a hard hug, which seemed to startle him. He almost let go of his pole. "See you next Friday!" she sang. She turned to me. "I'll call you!"

"Okay," I sang back, hoping she heard the sarcasm. Addison never called me to chat. She called when she needed something.

"Keep your nose clean," she added, touching the tip of her nose, before she disappeared through the door.

Carter gave me a curt nod. "See ya."

I nodded back. *I can't wait.*

As the doors shut behind them, I swung around my pole, into the nearest empty seat. The train had cleared out. There was lots of space now. The people in my neighborhood did not use public transportation.

Max sat right beside me, dragging his football bag with him. I moved my baton bag to one side so it didn't poke him in the thigh. I looked out the far window of the train so I didn't say something else stupid and give away how fast my heart raced at how close he was. We spent a short stint below ground. The lights flashing by on the tunnel wall were the only indicators that we were moving. Then we climbed into the sunset, with the skyscrapers of Buckhead peeking above the trees and coming closer.

"You didn't really think you'd ruined my mojo, did you?"

I jumped a little at the sound of his voice.

"You looked worried," he said. "Carter was kidding."

Max was *so cute*. But he'd asked Addison out, so I knew he wasn't flirting with me. Max and I were friends. I could relax. RELAX, GEMMA.

I loosened my shoulders against the back of the seat and raised my eyebrows skeptically. "So you *don't* really wear the same underwear every game?"

He smiled. "Yeah, I do."

"And you're *not* worried that a chick from the opposing team said you would get your ass kicked?"

He laughed. "Well, okay, but I don't want you to feel bad about it. You didn't know I have a problem. And you're from the opposing team, after all. You should be glad if I lose my mojo."

"I watched you at camp, Max." This was hard for me to do, but I held his gaze, even as the MARTA rumbled over a connection in the track and rocked back and forth. I messaged to him that I thought I'd seen *him* watching *me*.

His brows dipped briefly, like he wondered what I was getting at.

"You don't miss," I told him.

He said just as seriously, "No, I don't."

I opened my hands. "Then why are you worried?"

A little movement in his cheek told me he'd been clenching his jaw. Finally he said, "I *have* to make every goal."

I nodded. "Because there's tension between you and Carter." Understatement of the year.

"There's tension between you and Addison, too," he said. "You seem like an unlikely pair. Are you friends because you're both majorettes?"

I took a breath, considering how to answer truthfully without prompting Addison to kill me. "When we were ten, I was pudgy." Might as well admit it, now that Addison had blown my cover. "Self-conscious. And Addison—"

Had a big mouth. Was mean and spiteful. Did not have many friends. Any true explanation I could have given him would get me in trouble with her. So I said, "Our mothers were majorettes together in high school."

"Really!" Max said.

"Yeah."

"Best friends?"

I had wondered this myself. "You know, I'm not sure how close they were." My mom planned a lot of balls for charity, where the movers and shakers in Atlanta could see and be seen, but she wasn't outgoing. She spent most of her time by herself.

"Anyway," I said, "our parents got divorced at about the same time." I stopped myself there. Addison wouldn't want me telling her date the uglier parts of her family background. So I left out that her dad had gone to trial for making a lot of questionable investments. At least he didn't go to jail, but a huge chunk of their money was gone.

"Our moms threw us together in majorette class," I said. "The nice thing about having a friend forced on you is, you're never alone."

"Yep." Max nodded as if he really understood what I meant. "So nowadays, when the two of you aren't getting along, you remember how you were able to talk to each other about your family problems back then. When you look at her, what you're really seeing is the girl you became friends with in the first place, and it's harder to get mad at her."

"Yyyyeah," I said slowly. This seemed sort of right. Addison and I had never talked about our family problems, as far as I remembered. We had never talked about much of anything. But I had spent the night at her house a lot during that turmoil, and I had enjoyed how loud and crazy it was with her older sister and younger brothers. She'd spent some nights at my house, and she'd probably enjoyed the silence that I hated so much. I had walked with her across the school yard while mean boys had yelled insults about her father's mug shot in the newspaper, and she had walked with me when boys said my red skirt was as big as a caboose.

"How about you and Carter?" I asked. "Are you friends because of football?" I doubted this, since football seemed to be a sore subject between them.

"We both moved to town when we were nine," he said. "I guess we found each other because we both were different. I was from California, and I'm Japanese, as you can see." He moved his hand down his body, presenting himself, *ta-da*. "And Carter's parents adopted him from Russia."

"Russia!" I exclaimed. "Like, the country?"

"No, Russia, Ohio."

I deserved that. *Russia, like, the country?* Good Lord. I'd made a clueless comment of Addison-esque proportions.

But Max seemed to like that. He'd asked her out, after all.

Then I second-guessed what Max had meant. Maybe he was serious. "Carter is from Russia, Ohio?"

Max rolled his eyes. "There's no Russia, Ohio."

That ticked me off. I was *not* as stupid as he seemed to think I was. "I'll bet there is." I unzipped my baton bag, pulled my phone from the side compartment, and got online. "Ha! It's thirty-four miles north of Dayton." I turned to him.

Again, he was closer than I expected, his face near my shoulder, leaning over to see my phone.

"You're speechless," I noted. "Probably for the first time all week."

He smiled more broadly and watched me.

We eyed each other so long that I was sure he was looking right through me and could tell how hard I'd fallen for my best friend's date.

I laughed nervously. "Carter's from *Russia*?" I repeated. "He doesn't have an accent."

"Yes, he does," Max said. "You're not listening. It's a lot

more subtle now than when he was nine, though. The kids at school made fun of him."

I winced, feeling sorry for nine-year-old Carter. "That's terrible."

"It was terrible when they made faces at me, too." With his fingers, Max lifted the outside corners of his eyes.

"Yep. It was terrible when my bra was two cup sizes bigger, and boys called me Gemma Van Cleavage."

I almost slapped my hand over my mouth. I could not *believe* I had said that to him. The problem with pretending to be extroverted was that once I started, there was no telling what would come out of my mouth.

But Max only laughed. "Yep." Then he eyed me again. "So, listen." At the last second, his gaze faltered. He looked down at his shorts and picked at a frayed spot on the hem. "What did Addison mean when she told you to keep your nose clean?"

Sure, I would tell him. I was taking a lot of perverse pleasure in making him realize he had chosen the wrong girl. I said without missing a beat, "She meant that I'd better not try to steal you from her."

5

"You'd better not steal me from Addison?" Max repeated, sounding confused.

"Yes, and she'd better not steal Carter from me, either." I pretended to ponder the possibility, as if such a misfortune would be very grave indeed. Then I laughed it off like I'd convinced myself I was being ridiculous. Dearest Addison would not steal my boyfriend!

"It's our coach's idea," I explained. "Mrs. Baxter." I said her name with my nose in the air. "She's a million years old, and she runs the majorette line in a very traditional way. That's not all bad. There are certain things we concentrate on, like following through with movements"—I reached my right arm in an arc as if I were holding a baton—"and putting our heads down when the baton goes down, and popping them up when the baton goes up." I showed him the proper head movements with my long ponytails flying around and tickling my neck. "If you're doing it right, you get your bouffant hairdo stuck in your tiara."

"Tiara!" he laughed, incredulous.

"Yes!" I said. "The thing is, judges at band contests are looking for this sort of old-school follow-through, so our majorette line gets terrific marks. But the downside is that Mrs. Baxter is old school in other ways too. She is *watching us*." I moved in and gave Max the evil eye just like Mrs. Baxter did.

"We're not supposed to steal each other's boyfriends or get in arguments in the lunchroom," I said. "We are supposed to behave like young ladies, and she had better not hear anybody talking about us behind our backs. She says we have to keep our noses clean, and when she says this, she actually touches her finger to her nose, just like Addison did." I repeated the gesture. "I guess I shouldn't have a problem with any of that. I'm not the boyfriend-stealing type."

"You're not?" he asked.

"No. Sorry." I patted his knee playfully and *wished* he really did look rueful.

"But I resent this old lady getting all up in my business," I said. "I just want to twirl, you know? She acts like we're role models for the rest of the school. I'm thinking . . . on what planet? We're dancing with batons in skimpy, glittery outfits in front of any lecher who pays for a ticket into the football stadium. We are the modern-day equivalent of the dance hall girl."

Honestly, I was still doing my extroverted act, trying to get through this awkward time with the guy my best friend had already claimed. I didn't expect him to be interested. Or to *converse* with me. When several seconds of silence passed, I figured he'd zoned out.

Then he said very seriously, "Football players get that role model speech too. When adults say shit like that, I guess they're thinking you're always a role model when you can do something that takes guts and concentration. Though I'm not sure why guts and concentration are so important in the adult world. It's like they want all of us to grow up to be high-rise construction workers."

I giggled. "Or dance hall girls!"

"Or something," he agreed.

"Anyway, we majorettes have to keep our noses extra clean for the next few weeks," I said, "because we have a vote coming up right after the first game—the game we play against you guys—to see who will be next year's head majorette."

"And you're up for head majorette?" he prompted me.

Me? "Yeah, technically, Addison and a girl named Delilah and I are all up for it. We're the only three rising juniors on the majorette line. The rest are seniors. It has to be one of us. It's definitely not going to be me. Delilah has stage fright. Addison isn't worried. She'll get it for sure."

"And you don't want it?" he asked.

I should have said no. Instead, I shrugged, as if the answer might be yes. I had no idea why I did that. The vote for head majorette was just another popularity contest, this time among the majorettes rather than the whole school. I didn't want to win a popularity contest over Addison. I didn't care at all. Did I?

But because I didn't give Max a firm negative, he looked at me probingly for another long moment. Then he asked, "What are your duties as head majorette?" Funny, he phrased it as if I were actually going to get this position.

And as I described it to him, for the first time I pictured myself in the role. "I would stand in the middle of the football field and twirl my baton on the fifty yard line, while my fellow majorettes were banished to the forty-five and the forty and the thirty-five. And whereas all the other majorettes would wear a blue sequined leotard, I would wear a white one, appearing to glow like a gargantuan pearl, which is what every girl dreams of. I would greet the visiting band officers during games along with the drum major of the band, the drum captain, the flag captain, and so forth. I would be an ambassador of the baton, if you will."

Max laughed a deep belly laugh as he coughed out, "But why do you vote *this* year for *next* year's head majorette?"

"Well, you're the head majorette–elect. You watch the current head majorette and learn from her. The rest of the junior majorettes have to try out again in the spring to make the squad for their senior year, but the head-elect automatically gets on the squad."

Max grinned. "Like on a reality show? She's granted immunity and can't be voted off the island?"

"Exactly!" I exclaimed. "And there's a reason. If we didn't have a head-elect who was immune, it's conceivable that when Addison, Delilah, and I tried out next spring, none of us would make it. An entirely different set of girls could be on the squad. So you'd have a whole team of first-year majorettes, and nobody would know what was going on. Mrs. Baxter wants somebody with experience to help her out."

"That makes sense."

"Yeah. But it's not fair. We perform at one game and vote for head majorette at the end of it. It's just a popularity vote—and a continuation of the whole tryout process. Did you know we had to do a routine in front of the whole school? Most of the people voting for us had no idea how good or bad we were. They were voting only for how we looked. It's a miracle I made the line." I shook my head, thinking back to that awful day last April. "I was heavier then, and I lost sleep over it. Judging people on how they look isn't fair."

He put his elbow on his thigh and his chin in his hand and leaned way forward, examining me. "It may not be fair," he said slowly, "but it's life. Try being the Japanese guy going out for the football team."

"At least the whole school isn't watching you and voting you up or down," I pointed out.

"I feel like they are, every time I attempt a kick." As he said this, he shifted his hand over his mouth like he was uncomfortable.

I reached out to touch his hand and pull it away from his mouth. I was so focused on him that it didn't occur to me how personal the move was until I did it and he gazed at me with those dark eyes.

Determined not to show my embarrassment, I reassured him, "Every time you *make* a kick."

He swallowed. "Right." A weird moment ticked by as we held hands—like I'd suddenly become the self-assured one, and he needed the boost.

We both jumped as the train doors slid open.

"We're here," he murmured vaguely, grabbing his bag

from the floor. I didn't say so, but following him off the train, I felt just as disoriented as he was acting. My hand tingled where it had touched his warm hand.

A few other passengers got off the train with us and immediately disappeared up the stairs to the parking deck. The train moved out of the station while Max and I stood there awkwardly on the platform, facing each other.

Finally he motioned toward the stairs with his head and said, "I'm parked in the deck. Are you?"

"My mom's coming to get me," I said. "I'm not sixteen yet."

"Oh, you're just a baby!"

This was such a weird thing for a boy to say. But his whole face lit up when he said it, until I laughed along.

"But you said you'll be a junior?" he asked.

"Yeah. I'm turning sixteen in three weeks."

"From today?"

"From yesterday."

His brows knitted for a moment like he was filing this information away for later. "So you're just young for our class."

"Pretty much." I hated it, too. I couldn't wait until I got my license. I wouldn't have to rely on anybody for a ride again.

Except . . . I was beginning to look forward to Max picking me up for my date with Carter.

"Well." He shifted his football bag to his other hand. "Why don't I drive you home?"

"Um." I wanted so badly for him to drive me home. But I wanted more than that from him. I wanted a chance with him. And that awful feeling of longing coupled with doom was exactly how I'd felt about Robert for the last two years.

When I didn't answer, Max asked, "Is that creepy? I don't fit the profile of a serial killer, you know."

I laughed. "That is what all serial killers say. That's how they draw their victims in."

"Good point."

"No, it's just that my mom's already on her way."

He plopped his bag down between his feet, holding it by the strap, and cocked his head at me. He looked adorable that way, with his hair hanging longer on one side. "Can I wait with you until your mom comes?"

YES. "You don't have to," I said. "It's not exactly a dangerous part of town."

"That's what all serial killer victims say. I would feel better."

A southbound train pulled in with a short honk and a spooky whine of rushing air. In the morning when I'd caught the MARTA, the skylights overhead had let in plenty of sun. In the evening, though, the light was fading, the station was deserted, and all the textured gray concrete with decorative metal scaffolding made the place about as inviting as a jail in space. I'd never felt uncomfortable on the train in the year my mom had let me ride it by myself, but I was glad to have Max with me. I supposed I could indulge him and let him wait with me.

"The street exit is this way," I said. We headed for the stairwell. After three flights down, we popped into the warm evening. A busy mall was just around the corner, but this area was quieter. We walked to the concrete bench at the pull-in where my mom would meet me.

As we sat down, Max asked, "Did Addison tell you I'm picking you up on Friday? I need your address."

Electricity rushed through my veins at his mention of picking me up . . . even though we'd be carpooling to his date with Addison.

"I'll text it to you." I fumbled in my baton bag for my phone. "What's your number?" As he recited it, I plugged in the digits. After I texted him, he peered at his own phone, then typed something. I thought he was recording my info, but a second later, I got a text:

Thank you Gemma!!!!!!!!!!!!!!!!!!!!!!!!

I laughed. It was nice that he even *pretended* to be enthusiastic about me. I would take it. "You're welcome."

As he tucked his phone back into his own bag, he asked offhandedly, "How'd you lose all that weight?"

I stared at him, wondering what he meant by *that*. Lots of people had grilled me about my weight since I started losing. Usually they asked me why I was giving in to the beauty queen mystique and trying to look like every other girl. But he seemed genuinely curious, nothing more. No agenda.

"I told my baton teacher what I wanted to do," I said. "She explained it to me in mathematical terms. If you take in more calories than you burn, you'll gain weight. If you take in less, you'll lose weight. I got on the Internet and figured out how many calories I was burning in a day. Then I added up what I was eating. Cobbler has a *lot* of calories."

"Cobb— Wow!" He laughed. "You were eating a lot of cobbler?"

"Yes. My mom makes it."

"Low-fat cobbler, or—"

"In Atlanta? God, no. That's your California roots talking. You probably make it with tofu out there."

He grinned and shrugged. "And sweetened with organic honey."

"Right. Around here it's refined sugar, lots of butter, and a scoop of full-fat ice cream on the side."

He winced. "Often? Every day?"

"At least. My mom is a great cook. I used to cook with

her, and we would eat together. And snack together. And have dessert together." I thought back to those nights when I'd felt warm and safe and way too full. "Sometimes we might have dessert together twice."

"I gotcha." As he said this, he chuckled a little. Not like he was making fun of me, but like he really did understand the rut my mom and I had gotten into after my dad left, and how hard it had been for me to get out.

"The other thing my baton instructor told me was to ask myself, 'Am I hungry? Or do I just want something to eat?' The answer with cobbler is always going to be that you just want some cobbler. You've already had dinner, so there's no way you can be hungry."

"I could be hungry," Max said.

"Really?" I looked at him beside me, his legs too long to sit comfortably on the concrete bench.

"Lately, yeah," he said.

"You're burning more calories playing football than I am twirling baton."

"Probably."

"I haven't gone on a weird diet," I said in my defense, because I always had to say this to Addison and Robert and everybody else who teased me. "I haven't even stopped eating my mom's cooking. I just eat less of it, and no cobbler, ever."

He looked up at the skyscraper in front of us rather than

at me as he asked, "How does your mom feel about that?"

"I really don't care," I grumbled. Total lie. I was afraid she felt like I had betrayed her. But I couldn't dwell too much on that, because I absolutely refused to go back to my previous weight. "I exercised, too, but that was easy because there's a gym at my house."

"You mean, your mom buys a piece of exercise equipment, thinking she will use it every day, and it gathers dust, and eventually she makes you move it into the spare room? My mom does that too. There's not much butter in Japan, and apparently she went hog wild when she first came to America. Butter, and then loaf bread, and then she discovered mayonnaise. She seemed to have gotten a handle on it, but then we moved to Atlanta and there were biscuits."

I laughed and said, "Just keep her away from the cobbler." But when I'd said there was a gym at my house, I hadn't meant my mom bought exercise equipment. I'd meant that my house contained a gym. It was a big house.

He must have read my mind. As a truck rumbled by, he turned to me and asked loudly over the noise, "So, your dad used to own part of the Falcons? Like, the wide receiver and a couple of tight ends?"

"More like half the cheerleaders, knowing him."

Instantly I wanted to take back that bitter joke. Max

was making polite conversation while we waited for my mom. He probably regretted it now.

He played along, though, scooting closer on the bench like he was interested in what I was saying. "That's why your parents got divorced?"

I nodded. "When I was ten. He and my mom were big on the country club, dinner party, charity ball scene, because it was good for his business. But then it got back to my mom that he had a girlfriend."

Max nodded.

"So now—it's kind of weird, if I think about it—they're both doing half of what they used to do. My dad moved to Hilton Head with his girlfriend, but he still runs all his businesses and makes a lot of money from there. My mom got the house, so she still throws huge dinner parties for charity. They just don't do it as a couple anymore."

"Did you realize that when you talk about this, your breathing speeds up?"

I held my breath, looking at Max. I had not realized this. But yes, my chest felt tight and my head hurt, and I swayed a little on the bench, slightly dizzy.

He reached toward my chest, like he was going to touch me.

His hand stopped in midair.

Two bright spots of pink appeared on his cheeks, apparent even in the fading light of dusk, and I felt my face coloring too.

He put his hand over his own heart. "Do this," he said.

I put my hand over my heart. It was racing. Talking about my dad made me anxious, but what made my heart race now was Max himself.

"There's my mom," I said quickly, recognizing her car at the intersection down the block. I did not add, *Damn it!* I wished she'd had something important to do and had been running late for once. I turned to Max to say good-bye.

He was staring at the car. Generally girls at my school thought it was a nice, expensive car, but boys knew exactly what it was and how much it had cost. Their faces showed admiration mixed with envy. Max wore the same expression as he asked, "Is that an Aston Martin?"

"Yeah," I said as casually as I could, pretending I didn't understand his astonishment. "It's six years old. Before my dad left, he wanted to make sure my mom had a safe, reliable car so she and I didn't get stuck somewhere with engine trouble, since he wouldn't be around to help anymore."

"He could have done that for a lot less money," Max said, eyes still on the car. "That is *not* why your dad bought your mom a car that cost six figures."

I glared at Max. I wasn't stupid. He was right, of course.

My dad had given my mom the house and bought her a ridiculously expensive car so she would feel special, could keep up her image, and would agree not to fight the prenup that prevented her from going after half of everything my dad had ever made. Sure. But just because it was true did not mean I wanted to discuss it with Max.

"I'm sorry," he backtracked immediately. "I shouldn't have said that."

"No, you shouldn't have," I said more loudly than I'd intended—loudly enough that I heard my words echoing against the concrete MARTA station curving around us. I was too angry to care. "You read people really well, Max, and I enjoy it up to a point, but you can't just blurt out everything you see."

He pointed at me. "Remember Addison asked me why I don't have a girlfriend? This is why."

I laughed shortly. "You do now."

As my mom stopped in the pull-off, the engine rumbling at our feet, he gave me a hard look. "You are a very interesting person, Gemma. Very different, in a good way." He stood, dragging his bag with him.

I tried to smile. "Do you want my mom to drop you off at your parking deck?"

He grinned. "Are you worried about my safety? That is really cute, Gemma."

"I'm serious. You were worried about *my* safety. That's why you're here."

His dark brows shot up. For the briefest moment, I wondered if that really *was* why he was here.

But of course it was. He shrugged. "Like you said, this is probably the safest place in Atlanta. And I look mean, don't I?"

He didn't look mean. His face was open and sweet, like the friendliest person I'd ever met. But he *was* at least six feet tall, which was probably what he meant.

If I admitted how daunting he'd look to a would-be attacker, I would sound like I liked him. I didn't want to insult him, though. So I asked, "Are we back on the serial killer thing again?"

He threw back his head and laughed. Then he put his hand on my shoulder. "See you next Friday night, Gemma."

And then, before I could react, he reached past me and opened the passenger door of my mom's car. I climbed in, dragging my baton bag after me. He closed the door with a thick *thud*.

As my mom drove away from the curb, I watched Max in the side mirror. He stood staring after us for a moment, looking straighter and thinner and taller now that I could see all of him, not just his expressive face. He shook his head as he slung his bag over his shoulder and walked up the sidewalk toward the parking deck.

"And who was that?" my mother asked expectantly. She stopped at the next intersection, by the mall and restaurants and high-rise hotels. Smiling couples held hands as they crossed the street in front of us.

Willing the tingle in my shoulder where he'd touched me to fade away, I sighed, "Max. Addison's date."

6

"*Addison's* date!" my mom exclaimed.

"Yep." I barreled through an explanation so she wouldn't ask me twenty questions. "He's a junior too, and he's a kicker for the football team at East. We met him today at Tech. His dad is a professor there. Max was in football camp while we were in majorette camp. Addison's going out with him next Friday, and I'm going out with his friend Carter, if that's okay with you, to a concert. Max is picking me up because he lives around here. He was just waiting with me until you came."

"That was nice of him," my mom said. She peered into the rearview mirror as if to give him another once-over, even though he was long gone. She looked out the windshield again. "He has such good manners."

"Yep," I said.

"He's very handsome," she said.

"Yep," I said.

I felt her watching me across the dark car. I'd never been on a date, but I'd assumed I would go on one now that I was a majorette and looked the part, except for my hair. Maybe my mom had been waiting for this too. She would have laughed if I'd explained to her how badly I wanted Max to be my date, and how far that was from happening.

She gave a little gasp. "What happened to your nose?"

I'd forgotten all about my injury after my nose had stopped throbbing. I touched it tenderly. It was sore. That's probably what Max had been staring at the whole time I thought he was looking right through me to my soul.

"Addison hit me with her baton," I said.

My mom raised an eyebrow but didn't comment. I had suffered many injuries at Addison's hands. Most of them had not been accidents, but I'd always claimed they were so I wouldn't lose my only friend.

I was having second thoughts about that policy.

"So, you ate at the Varsity?" my mom asked. "What'd you eat? Not what you ordered, but what you *ate*."

"A grilled chicken sandwich," I said. "I ordered it and I ate it."

"Is that all?" she exclaimed. "Are you still hungry? I made lasagna and kept it warm for you."

"That sounds so good," I said truthfully. "Maybe I'll have some tomorrow." But I knew tomorrow she would cook something else and press me to eat that. I couldn't eat everything. Not anymore.

"How about some fresh peach cobbler with vanilla bean ice cream?"

Now she had me. Sweets had always been my weakness. I mean, food in general had been my weakness, but dessert was the worst. My mouth watered at the thought of cold ice cream melting over the flaky brown crust, sugar sparkling in the light from the kitchen chandelier, and all those sweet peaches. Georgia was the Peach State, and peaches were in season. My mom and I would sit at the table together and eat and say *mmmmmm* and feel like a family.

But I couldn't do it. As I'd told Max, in the past nine months, I'd learned the difference between wanting food and being hungry. I was not hungry.

"Maybe tomorrow," I repeated.

My mom was quiet, probably thinking about whatever charity ball she was planning at the moment. My thoughts drifted to our over–air-conditioned mansion ahead.

After the day I'd had with Addison, it was ridiculous of me to miss her. Yet I felt a horrible dread as my mom turned onto our street, passed the Campbells' house and the Browns' and the Khans', and pulled into our brick driveway. If Addison were driving me home, she would be blasting the sickly sweet pop station specifically because she knew I hated it. But when she parked in my driveway, I never wanted to get out of her car. Addison was rude, selfish, and spiteful. She was also full of life, and she made noise.

My mom parked in the spotless garage with three of the four spaces empty, and sighed. "I have a lot of work to do tonight, honey. A *lot*. But when I get through, I want to hear all about majorette camp and these boys."

"Okey-doke." I unlocked the door into the kitchen and galloped upstairs. My mom promised all the time that we'd chat, then got absorbed in what she was doing. She'd be working until I fell asleep. She would not ask me about camp. Neither of us would say anything for the rest of the night.

I closed the door of my room and waited for her to get her cobbler and ice cream and shut herself in her office, so I wouldn't be tempted. When the coast was clear, I unzipped my bag, took out my batons, and ran back downstairs, through the kitchen where the scent of peaches and sugar still hung in the air. I let myself out the French door, into the hot, humid night, a relief after the supercooled air inside the house. I crossed the marble patio to the big back lawn.

One of the instructors at camp had advised us first-time majorettes that the biggest hazard of our halftime show would be the bright stadium lights. If we weren't careful, we would toss up a baton, lose it in the glare of the lights, and drop it. In the band formation I would be in front of the student section. I could *not* drop a baton. Facing the spotlight on the corner of the roof, I threw baton after baton into the glare and practiced catching them by feel instead of by sight, until my hands were sore. And then kept going.

I didn't see Addison for the rest of the weekend. She was doing charity work for her debutante ball, which was coming up in October. Most people understood the debutante ball as a place where rich girls made a lot of affected movements and got "presented" to the rich boys who went to the same country club. All of that was true, but the girls needed community service hours too. It was kind of like training to become my mother, so when they turned forty-five, they too could be single mothers, live alone in a mansion, and plan charity balls for other people. That's what I called living.

I guess it was kind of strange that Addison was a debutante and I wasn't. Addison's mom was stretching to scrape up the money. They lived in what was jokingly referred to as the "slum" of this part of Atlanta, which meant the houses were made of brick, not marble, and had four bedrooms instead of fourteen. But Addison's mom was still trying to make up to society for her embezzling husband.

And me, I'd never wanted to be a debutante. I'd been overweight when I had to decide. I didn't want that kind of attention. I probably would have had to dye over the streaks in my hair. It just wasn't who I was. Astonishingly, my mom had brought up the idea only once. And unlike Addison bullying me into things, when I said no, my mom had let it go.

So a lot of weekends without Addison stretched before me. I felt a mix of relief that I wouldn't have to put up with her, and stir-craziness that there wouldn't be any driving around town looking for Hot Male Action (by which Addison meant whistling to boys shooting hoops at the park). The silence in my house was broken only by the sound of my mom tapping on the computer keyboard in her office, which echoed down the hall and around the marble stairwell. I could only stay so long outside in the ninety-five-degree heat, practicing baton.

Finally, on Sunday afternoon, I asked my mom to drop me off at the library while she ran some errands. This branch sat between Max and Carter's high school and mine. I figured it would have their high school yearbook from last May.

I was right. I snagged it from the shelves. I told myself I was only making sure that Max and Carter were who they said they were, and that they had not in fact been attending serial killer camp at Georgia Tech. I could have looked them up online, but social pages were easy to fake. I was smarter than that. I had to protect Addison, because she was too trusting to say no to any handsome stranger who asked her out. Or too horny.

The thought of Addison being horny for Max made me so tense that I accidentally ripped a page as I turned it. I took a deep breath to calm down, and looked around to make sure a librarian wasn't about to kick me out for destroying the collection.

I thumbed through to the football team pages and found Max and Carter in the junior varsity group photo. They were also in the varsity photo. Lots of varsity teams dressed out their junior varsity players in case the juniors and seniors got hurt, and to make the team look bigger and more menacing. The boys' faces were so small in both photos that I wouldn't have recognized them except for their names in the fine print. To make sure they hadn't looked up a couple of real students and given Addison and me false names in an elaborate serial killer ploy, I paged through to the individual pictures of last year's sophomore class.

Kichirou Maximilian Hirayama. That was Max all right, with an expression of utter joy on his face, like the photographer had told him history's funniest joke. I smiled just looking at him.

I flipped several more pages. *Carter Nelson.* He frowned. I'd seen similar expressions of the faces of starting football players in high school game programs, but usually not in their yearbook pictures. Their girlfriends would complain. Nobody wanted to look at that.

Another photo caught my eye as I thumbed through last year's sophomores. Max was seated at what appeared to be a lunchroom table, surrounded by other students, with an open box in front of him. It must have been his birthday. Ribbon and paper were scattered across the table. He had that same look on his face, that deep-down happiness. All the other kids in the picture were laughing too. Maybe one of these beautiful girls had been his girlfriend back then, and she felt so warm inside because she'd bought him the perfect gift.

Wow, I was imagining *way* too much. I would need to be careful when I saw Max next Friday so I didn't let it slip that I'd seen this picture and wondered about his life outside the Varsity and the MARTA system. I would seem like a stalker.

For that reason, I didn't thumb through the yearbook anymore, even to search for his picture in club photos to find out what his hobbies were. Any knowledge like that would give away my crush. I had made a mistake like that when Robert left his schedule on the lunchroom table where I could see it at the beginning of school last year. I had memorized it, and later I had made a point of walking very slowly by his classes. My crush was so painfully obvious that he had cornered me on a band trip and stressed to me that he wanted to be *just friends*, as if he was afraid the other trumpets would find out I liked him and make fun of him for it. Mortifying!

It was better that I didn't know too much about Max. The less I knew, the less I needed to forget. I closed the book and considered running the hem of my T-shirt along it to wipe off my fingerprints. I reshelved it without any crime scene cover-up and went outside to meet my mom.

A few minutes before Max was supposed to pick me up on Friday, I sat on the front porch to wait for him. My house was imposing. Grandiose. Embarrassing. I thought hanging out on the steps in my rock band T-shirt and shorts might lessen the impact of the thick polished marble columns and the fourteen-foot-tall windows.

Also, I did not want Max to ring the doorbell. My dad

had a gag bell installed that sounded like a gong in a palace. It was a joke. I didn't think it was funny. I'd complained about it to my mom, but she didn't know how to change the sound, and she'd never bothered to hire someone to fix it.

When Max pulled into the brick driveway in the longest old clunker I had ever seen, I crossed the lawn to meet him. But I stopped short and did a double take when he unfolded his tall frame from the car. He'd grown a goatee. I thought he'd been cuter clean shaven. Fresh-faced and younger-looking.

But as I considered him, I decided maybe "cute" was not my favorite look for him anyway. "Cute" had gotten my attention in the first place, but mature and handsomely devilish-looking would definitely *keep* my attention. Of course, it didn't matter whether he had my attention or not. He was dating Addison, so he would never know.

7

As I stood there in the hot evening sunshine, brushing away the gnats I'd stirred up in the grass, I felt the most profound sadness. Max's goatee had surprised me because I hadn't seen him in a week. I had missed six days of his classmates teasing him about the awkward, in-between, you-really-need-to-shave phase as his goatee grew in. It was just facial hair this time, but our lives had so little to do with each other, really. He could lose a leg and it would be a week before I found out.

Squinting against the sunlight, he backed against the car door to close it. "Hi. Do I look foreign in this?"

"Um," I said, trying to puzzle out what he was talking

about. The goatee didn't make him look foreign. Just older. "What?"

"Sometimes people take one look at me and start speaking. Very. Slowwwwwwwly. Like I can't understand English."

I examined his gray plaid shorts, which might have looked nerdy on another boy but were part of Max's effortless ultracool look, along with his tight red T-shirt and his long hair. Finally I said, "You don't *stand* foreign."

"Really? How do I stand?" He assumed a weight-lifter pose, flexing his biceps for me.

I laughed it off and tried not to ogle him. "You stand like an American high school football kicker."

He relaxed and put his fists on his hips. "But do I *look* foreign? It must be the hair."

Okay, his hair *was* a little too stylish to blend in around here, but that wasn't what caught my attention now that I considered him in this new way. "Your T-shirt is written in Japanese."

He pulled his T-shirt away from his chest with two fingers and examined it. "I hadn't thought about that. We visit my grandparents in Japan every year. I buy a lot of T-shirts because they're so different from what you can get in America."

"So you *do* want people to notice you," I pointed out.

He opened his mouth. Closed it again.

"I understand," I assured him. "You want people to notice you, but on your own terms."

He frowned at me.

To change the subject in case he was as sensitive about that as he seemed, I asked, "What does your T-shirt say, anyway?"

"Dunno. I always have to ask my mom. She tells me they all say, 'Bullshit.'"

"Bullshit!" I sputtered laughter.

"Her English is good but not nuanced," he explained. "Sometimes she changes it up with another word she's learned, like 'whackadoodle.' She'll do this." He pointed at two characters in a line on his shirt and pronounced two syllables with each. "'To-mo, da-chi.'" He underlined them with his finger. "'Whackadoodle.'"

Carefully I wiped away the tears under my eyes so as not to smear my makeup. "She sounds funny."

"She is funny. Just . . ." He rolled his eyes. "Foreign."

"What does your dad say?"

Max shrugged. "He thinks my struggles are amusing and futile." I was pretty sure that was a direct quote from his dad. Max's dark eyes got a faraway look, and he was quiet, which was rare for him.

"Well," I forced myself to say. "Welcome to my humble house."

He grinned as he walked toward me. "What house?" He pretended to do a double take and see the mansion for the first time, like I'd done for his goatee. "Oh! I didn't even notice it until you mentioned it."

If Addison were here, she would shove him playfully. I was afraid I might shove him off balance and kill him. And he wasn't my date. He was hers. So I just smiled, which probably made him think I didn't appreciate his sense of humor. I couldn't win. Finally I managed, "I'm sorry, but my mom says she has to talk to you before she will let Addison and me in your car."

"I figured she would."

"You already impressed her when you opened the car door for me at the MARTA station, so the interrogation shouldn't be too bad."

"Good to know." He gestured to the house, *ladies first*, and followed me inside.

My mom met us in the foyer, shook Max's hand, and led him into the library. Surrounded by dark paneled wood and thousands of books shelved floor to ceiling with a rolling ladder to get them down, and facing my mom, Max probably considered this the most awkward moment of his life.

But he sat in one of the leather chairs like it was a metal folding chair at school and talked animatedly to my mom like she was Addison or Carter or me. Either he was the only person I'd ever met who was comfortable with anyone in any situation, or it didn't occur to him to be embarrassed because the stakes for impressing my mom weren't very high. After all, he wasn't dating *me*.

He was only my ride to my first date ever.

"Nice wheels," I said a few minutes later, slipping into Max's car.

He closed my door, jogged around the hood, and sat on the driver's side. As he turned the key in the ignition, he said, "Very funny."

"I'm serious! What do you call a car like this?"

"I call it a 1983 Oldsmobile, on a good day. On a bad day I have a different name for it entirely."

"Did you buy it yourself?"

"Do you *think* I would pay my own money for this? My dad was going to buy me a new car. Then we got into an argument about Japanese versus classic American automotive technology, and he bought me this instead."

"Oooh. So you should never get in an argument with your father."

"I should never get in an argument with him about cars when he's planning to buy me a car. But this arrangement will only last until I break down on I-85." He winked at me. "Maybe then he'll buy me an Aston Martin."

"Oh, snap."

He raised his eyebrows at me, checking my expression. "I was kidding."

"I laughed."

He smiled. I could tell he felt bad about the joke and was trying to rein himself in, because his next question was sweet. "How's your nose?"

I touched it gingerly. "Still there." I'd hardly thought about it when Max and Carter weren't staring at me anymore.

"Good. First week of school treat you okay?"

"Band practice was great. We just work on our majorette routine for the whole hour every day. I can't believe I get a credit for that."

I didn't tell Max about the drama. Mrs. Baxter had dumbed down the routine because Addison and one of the seniors couldn't keep up with all the tricks she'd planned. Then Addison had gotten so embarrassed that she'd asked me to work with her after school. I'd told her I couldn't because I had to teach a class of fourth graders at the baton studio. She'd gotten mad.

"That sounds fun," Max said diplomatically.

"Yeah. And I switched my schedule around at the last minute. Our school has a great dance program that I never took advantage of before. I guess making majorette finally gave me the confidence to enroll in dance." I left out that I'd always wanted to take my school's dance classes, but there was no way. Every one of them required at least two public performances. In a leotard. I'd taken music classes instead.

I also left out that I hadn't informed Addison of my decision beforehand. When she'd found out I wasn't in music comp with her like I usually was, she'd gotten mad.

"That's good," Max said.

"I hope. And I'm getting a lot of attention for dating Carter."

Max stopped at an intersection and turned to face me. "What kind of attention?"

I shrugged. "You know."

He continued to watch me, which was frustrating. Max had seemed like a person I didn't have to explain things to. He usually knew what I meant, or acted like he did. That's why he was fun to talk with. Now that he was pressing me to be specific, talking with him wasn't fun. I racked my brain for an answer that wouldn't be embarrassing.

There wasn't one.

I said slowly, "Attention in general. I never got any before."

"I find that hard to believe."

"It's just because I'm a majorette now, and I'm going

out with the rival football team's quarterback. It's something for people to gossip about."

In fact, I had heard a rumor that Robert had gotten jealous of Carter and was planning to ask me out. It hadn't happened yet, but I had caught Robert staring at me a few times in band when I'd performed spin-turns he wasn't expecting. Funny how I would have been so excited about that four months ago. I would have checked my cell phone twenty times a day, hoping he would text me. But after he'd been so unsupportive during majorette tryouts and spent a whole summer pretending I didn't exist, I'd gotten to the point that I didn't miss Robert at all.

And now that I'd met Max, it was difficult to remember why Robert had ever seemed like the perfect guy for me.

Just my luck.

"Are they gossiping about Addison going out with the rival football team's kicker?" Max asked.

"Not so much," I said truthfully. Addison had gotten mad about this, too. In fact, as we'd walked around school together, people had stopped to ask me about Carter a *lot* more than they'd talked to Addison about Max. She might be having second thoughts about which boy she'd chosen.

That was okay. Tonight she'd have a great time with Max. Carter could continue to test how long he could go without saying anything. Or anything *nice.* And Addison would realize that she'd chosen the better man after all.

Max was still frowning at me.

"Bless your heart." I patted his bare knee playfully and tried to ignore the fact that his muscular leg was as hard as a rock. "*I* appreciate you, Max. *I* think you're gossip-worthy. Now drive."

Obediently he faced forward and accelerated through the four-way stop, but a worried crease remained between his brows. He was disturbed that Addison hadn't gotten as much social mileage out of dating him as I'd gotten out of dating Carter. He *should* be disturbed. It served him right for asking her out instead of me, because I certainly wouldn't have let something like that bother *me* if *I* were his date.

But I didn't want to argue with Max all the way to the shopping center where we were meeting Addison and Carter. I should make polite conversation and ask *Max* how *his* first week of school was.

Before I could get the words out, he asked, "What made you decide to lose weight?"

Heat rushed to my face, as it always did when someone mentioned my weight. It took me a few seconds to remember that there wasn't anything to feel self-conscious about now.

A second wave of blush hit my face as I realized why he was asking. He had met my mother. While I had lost weight, she had kept gaining. By now the contrast between us was getting pretty noticeable.

The silence had stretched so long that most people would backtrack and retract the question, thinking they had offended me. Not Max. He shot me a quick, expectant glance. I reminded myself that he was not Robert. Robert asked questions to embarrass me and put me in my place. Max asked questions because he liked me and was interested.

I swallowed. "Addison wanted to try out for majorette. She wanted me to do it too because she thinks she can't do anything by herself."

Okay, Max was my friend. He had not asked me out, but he didn't mind spending time with me. I would ruin that if I kept taking potshots at his date, who was supposed to be my dearest compadre.

I cleared my throat. "I don't know why Addison feels that way. Anyway, she said if I told her no, it would be because I didn't want to be seen in the majorette uniform at that weight. So . . ."

Max was supposed to take that as my answer and change the subject. But he stayed quiet. He was telling me I wasn't done.

And I realized that I wasn't. "She's made comments

about how I looked the whole time we've been friends, as if I didn't know how much I weighed and needed to have it pointed out."

Great, I was insulting his date again. I backtracked, "Of course, she was only trying to help. And this time, something clicked with me. I *didn't* want to wear the uniform. I didn't even want to *try out*. So I lost some weight. I tried out. I made it. And then I really was going to have to wear the uniform, so I lost the rest of the weight."

"Why didn't you just tell Addison no?" Max asked.

It was a reasonable question. But I felt violated when he asked it, like he had stepped over a line between friendly conversation and invasion of privacy. I said, "I don't tell Addison no."

"Why not?"

Because she's all I have.

I turned to the passenger window. We drove down a winding, tree-lined road with strictly manicured lush lawns on either side. There wasn't much to hold my interest as silence filled the car. The radio tuned to Album 88 wasn't loud enough to be distracting. Reaching down to turn up the volume would have seemed rude, something I would have done to escape an awkward silence with Carter. *Not* with Max.

"When are you going to stop?" Max asked.

When are you going to stop crushing on me? I went cold with panic. By degrees I realized that wasn't what he was talking about. "When am I going to stop losing weight?" I guessed.

"Yes. Addison said you've already lost fifty pounds."

"Forty-eight," I said without thinking. I cringed internally. *Thanks again, Addison, for putting the forty-eight-pounds-heavier Gemma into Max's head!* I said carefully, "I'm not judging by how much weight I've lost. I'm judging by the result."

"I'm *asking* you about the result." He glanced at me across the car, his long hair swinging into his eyes. He shook it away and said, "You're not still trying to lose, are you? It seems like you'd just be maintaining at this point."

"I am so *sick* of people trying to get me to stop!" I said more loudly than I'd meant to. My own voice rang in the car, an upper-class debutante-type harangue with the punk beat on the radio as a sarcastic background. All the frustration I'd felt for months came spilling out. "I used to eat whatever I wanted, whenever I wanted. It was *good.* It was incredibly hard for me to stop doing that. On top of that, I work out *every single day* and then practice baton for at least another hour. I am proud of myself. I feel better physically. I don't get tired when I twirl like I used to. I have accomplished something here. And all Addison and my mother can do is put milkshakes and peach cobbler in front of me and tell me to eat because I look anorexic, when I don't! I know I don't."

"Yeah, Addison commented on what you were eating when we were at the Varsity."

And you still asked her out? There was no accounting for taste.

He ran one hand back through his hair. "I know that's hard, and I know you've accomplished something. I also think there's a point where you stop losing weight in a healthy way, and it becomes an obsession. I've played football for years, and I've shared the locker room with the guys on the wrestling team."

I knew what he was getting at. Wrestling was huge around here—not as important as football, but still popular—and boys competed by weight class, which was decided when they got on the scale right before a meet. To have the best chance of winning, they wanted to be as muscular as possible, but weigh as little as possible, and I'd heard some of them resorted to drastic measures.

"I'm not bulimic or anything like that," I assured him. "I haven't thrown up since I caught the flu in the sixth grade. Addison and my mom have said that to me too, like that's the only way to lose weight."

"I don't mean that at all," he said. "I'm not talking

about now. I mean in the future." Max flipped on his turn signal. While we waited for the light to change, he reached one muscular arm across the car.

I thought he would put his hand on my shoulder, as he had when my mom picked me up from the MARTA last Friday. Instead, he touched my chin with one finger. He held me there gently and made sure I was listening to him. "If you don't have a goal, Gemma, you will never reach it."

My whole body vibrated from his touch, and from the realization that he was right. For the past nine months, I'd arranged my life around losing weight. What *was* my goal?

"You can get to the point that losing weight itself is the goal," he said, "and that's where you get into trouble. But you could stop here, today, and say, 'This is my goal. I don't need to lose any more weight. I have made it.' Wouldn't that be a huge burden lifted off your shoulders?"

I took a long breath, considering. "I enjoy working out. It's part of my day now, something I look forward to. And I love practicing baton. This is the first time I've ever felt like an athlete, and I don't want to stop."

"So don't stop. You *are* an athlete. Keep being an athlete. Your goal now isn't to change your body, but to keep the great body you have."

Max had said I had a great body. Last week Carter had

called me beautiful, and it had hardly registered. But Max's words echoed in my head.

I reminded myself that he was saying that as a friend, my best friend's date. *My* date's best friend. I knew this. So I concentrated on what he was really telling me. "It *would* be a relief to stop buying shorts."

"And you look great in those shorts," he said. "You look—"

He stopped talking and put his hand down. I couldn't blame him. Having me gape at him in the middle of his sentence was probably somewhat disconcerting.

As the turn signal tick-tocked the seconds away, he watched me with his dark eyes. He swallowed. "—great in those shorts," he repeated.

The light changed. He swung his car into the parking lot, where Addison and Carter were waiting for us in Carter's pickup. As we pulled in, they both got out of the truck to greet us.

Addison's top was cut so low that I was almost embarrassed for her. I would have been, if she hadn't been enjoying the attention. Every man who walked past her in the parking lot turned and looked. A group of boys our age even nudged one another and nodded in her direction. I could not *believe* her mother had let her out of the house in that—and then I saw the sweater tied around her waist.

Clearly she'd left the house with the sweater covering her boobage. Ruefully I looked down at my chest, most of which I had lost along with the forty-eight pounds. Gemma Van Cleavage was no more, but I did not miss her.

My outfit went in another direction entirely. I had made damn sure that what I wore would tell Max what kind of girl I was. *I* was the quirky one. Since my bracelet collection had not made this obvious to him before, I had worn my necklace collection instead, and I'd touched up the purple in my hair with an even more vibrant shade.

I might have miscalculated. I had assumed Max was that rare boy who *preferred* the quirky friend, and that he'd mistaken Addison's ditzy qualities for her free spirit. But when I saw the way he looked at her as we got out of his car, I knew he'd gotten what he'd asked for.

8

Without another word, I bailed out of the front seat of Max's car to make room for his date. Addison edged around the car door and squeezed past me into the passenger seat. I eyed her bare boobs and whispered, "Really?"

"Really!" She grinned her majorette grin. Sometimes I wondered whether Addison was all there. She didn't know when she was being made fun of. But this time she knew exactly what I was talking about. She jerked the door closed behind her. Through the window, I could see her leaning across the seat and giving Max a big hug hello, positioning herself so he could see down what little there was of her shirt.

"Hi," I called to Carter over the roof of the car.

"Hi," he said without smiling.

We both got into the backseat. With Addison and Max laughing together in the front, it seemed like Carter and I should . . . hug? Shake hands? Even a peck on the cheek would have been appropriate. But he looked out his window at the parking lot.

Finally he called impatiently into the front seat, "What's the plan, Max?"

"We're close to the mall," Max said. "Let's go make fun of rich people." He turned all the way around in the driver's seat, gasped as if he hadn't realized I was there, and said, "Oh—Gemma—I beg your pardon."

His teasing didn't bother me. Only Addison bothered me, laughing way more heartily than the joke called for.

"Ha-ha," I told him. "You can test all your jokes on me and see if I wither in pain."

His brows knitted ever so briefly, like he wasn't sure whether I could really take a joke or not. His eyes slid to Carter.

Then he turned around and started the car. "We'll skip the mall this time. I know a pizza place near the concert." He maneuvered the car out of the parking lot and back into traffic.

The radio had been a normal background volume in the front seat, but it was very loud in the back—so loud that

Carter and I couldn't have talked without shouting. But I didn't ask Max to turn it down, because I couldn't think of anything to say to Carter anyway. Every so often, Addison's cackle would rise above the music. I would catch her putting her hand on Max's shoulder or touching his goatee.

At least the scenery was interesting. Most of my life was spent bopping back and forth from home to school to the mall to home, with an occasional outing with Addison when she wanted to go trolling for boys. I didn't often ride the interstate through downtown. The highway was tucked so close to the buildings that I felt like I could almost reach out and touch them.

Just east of the city we took an exit into a gorgeous neighborhood of towering oak trees and restored Victorian homes, each painted five shades of purple or cream. Max parked on a quiet street.

"This is a long way to walk, Max," Carter grumbled as he got out of the car. He probably had two-a-day football practices, but he complained about a little walk?

Max glanced up the shady street lined with cars. "I could keep looking around, but more people will park here, and we'll just have to move farther away. That's how it is here on Friday night. I guess it *is* a long walk, though, depending on your shoes. Heel check."

Max stood in front of me, but he hadn't said anything

to me for the entire ride, so it took me a moment to realize that he was talking to me. I raised one foot to show him. He examined my shoe. "You're good. Very sensible, Gemma."

He looked at Addison. "Heel check." She showed off her high-heeled sandal. Max shook his head. "Not sensible at all, Addison. You're going to have to ride."

He turned around on the sidewalk, and she hopped up on his back. They turned to me like a two-headed monster and waited.

I stared for another moment, not knowing what they wanted. "Oh." I shut my door. Max stepped forward and locked the car with an actual key. Then he bounced Addison into a more comfortable position on his back and started up the sidewalk.

I fell in beside them, just so I wouldn't have to lag behind with silent Carter. "How do you know this neighborhood so well?" I asked Max.

"I drive around," he said. "I used to go exploring on the MARTA before I got my driver's license."

"Really!" I exclaimed. I was jealous. My mother would never have let me do that. When I rode the MARTA, I needed a specific destination and a well-lighted walk the whole way. And I was jealous of whatever girl he'd taken with him. "Not alone, I guess?"

"Yes, alone," Max sighed.

"Whether he parks or rides the MARTA, there's always a long walk." Carter grumbled behind us. "Who would want to go with him?"

I would, I thought. I would have loved to get lost in Atlanta with Max, walking through old neighborhoods, exploring shops off the beaten path, grabbing coffee at some place he knew.

But I could not have that, and wanting it would just make me more dissatisfied. I slowed a little until I was walking beside Carter. As I stepped behind Max and Addison, I could *feel* myself being absorbed into Carter's bubble of unhappiness.

I took a long breath through my nose, inhaling the scent of summer flowers, and admired the houses along the way. Someday maybe I would have one of these—a pretty house I'd restored myself, something beautiful for my friends to admire, but not so monstrous that it scared them away.

The farther we walked up the sidewalk, the more we passed other people walking. By the time we reached the first shops at Little Five Points, the sidewalks were packed with college-age kids and teenagers. Max stopped and put Addison down. I walked a little faster, not because I wanted to catch up with them or get away from Carter, but because the scene in front of me filled me with energy: a crowd, bright clothes, bright storefronts, booming music, and laughter. I cheered up, hardly caring that Carter hadn't spoken since we'd left the car.

"Look, a whole store for Gemma!" Addison exclaimed, pointing through the window of the shop we were passing. The mannequins wore striped stockings like the ones I'd worn to majorette tryouts, cool T-shirts, and leather—but other mannequins wore a more risqué version of punk, which was not me at all. Addison was trying to embarrass me. But I wouldn't let her. I grinned through it.

"No," I heard Max say, "that's what Gemma *would* wear if she really meant it."

I stopped short on the sidewalk, feeling my jaw tighten with anger. Carter and Addison kept walking, but Max noticed I was missing and turned to look for me. When he saw my face, his eyes widened. He knew he had crossed a line this time.

He ran two steps to catch up with Addison and Carter and said something to them. They looked back at me, but then stayed where they were and started talking. Carter had thought of something to say, now that he was not saying it to *me*.

Then Max jogged back down the sidewalk and nudged me to the side, out of the way of other pedestrians, against the punky shop window. He looked down at me and said, "Don't do that."

"Do what?" I grumped.

"You're going to turn sullen and stop talking for the rest of the night."

He was right, but I wasn't going to admit it. Not when he'd *made* me turn sullen. "I'd already stopped talking," I pointed out.

"With you, there's regular quiet, and then there's sullen quiet," he said. "You and Carter are both like that."

If Max was trying to cheer me up, he wasn't doing a very good job. I didn't want to be like Carter.

Of course, Max's observation explained a lot. He wanted to be friends with both Carter and me. Maybe he even wanted me for a close friend, like Carter was his close friend, but Max wanted to date someone entirely different.

"Gemma." He glanced up the sidewalk. When he saw Carter and Addison weren't watching, he turned back to me and used his long middle finger to brush a strand of purple hair away from my eyes.

I stared stubbornly up at him, my face on fire where his finger had brushed me, and burning with anger at what he had said and the situation the three of them had dragged me into.

"We had that whole talk when we were alone in my car," he said, "and you didn't get mad. I made fun of you for being rich and it didn't bother you at all. Why are you getting mad now?"

"Because when we were alone, you were trying to be nice. It was just a joke. Your comment about my clothes was meant to hurt me. Why did you take a jab at me, Max?" He'd already made me crush on him and then asked out my best friend. He could not insult me too.

"It's true, though," he defended himself. "You want to look punk, but you don't live that lifestyle at all."

"Just because you think it does not mean you should say it. We have been over this."

He was nodding before I got all the words out. "You're right. I know. I shouldn't have said it. I'm sorry."

He was sorry, but he still hadn't acknowledged he'd taken a swing at me on purpose. Had he been trying to get a rise out of me? Why would he do that?

"Don't be mad, Gemma, okay?"

I sighed. He wasn't going to explain himself, and now Carter and Addison were watching us. "Okay."

"Say something funny."

"Something funny."

He pursed his lips, considering me. "Hmm. I'm not sure you're back. Work on it."

He placed his hand between my shoulder blades and pressed, pushing me into walking up the sidewalk with him. At his touch, tingles raced all the way down to my fingertips. I was so angry at myself for my body's reaction to his that I could have cried.

"The pizza place is around the corner," he whispered as we walked. "They have really good dinner salads with meat on them, so you feel like you've eaten something, but it's, you know, still a salad. Healthier than pizza. If that's what you wanted."

"Thank you!" I exclaimed. That was exactly what I wanted. Good food, and a distraction from how far I'd fallen for Max.

We'd reached Carter and Addison on the sidewalk. Carter frowned at Max. "I didn't catch what he said to you, Gemma, but I'm sorry on his behalf. Didn't I tell you he makes girls mad?"

Addison cackled and put her arm around Max's waist like that was the most ridiculous thing she'd ever heard.

"Yes, you did warn us." I forced a laugh. "It's okay. I'll stop listening." As if I didn't hang on Max's every word.

The restaurant was packed. My heart sank. I figured we'd have to wait forever for a table, which meant more non-conversation with Carter. Thankfully, the hostess found us a table in the corner quickly.

Maybe Max still felt bad for what he'd said, and he was trying to make it up to me. Maybe he just knew how to work a room. For whatever reason, he managed to keep the conversation going among all four of us until our food came, so I never had to rack my brain for something to say.

In fact, I felt so good after half an hour of the four of us being nice to one another, and with some avocado in my stomach, that I was able to do my part on the date by calling up Extroverted Gemma. "Addison said you guys ref soccer games on Saturdays and Sundays."

"Yeah," the boys said in unison, and they rolled their eyes in exactly the same way, which I found hilarious.

I said, "I take it you don't enjoy it."

"Well," Max said, looking at Carter.

"It can be dangerous," Carter said.

"Dangerous!" Addison exclaimed. "How? Do you have to break up fights in the men's league?"

Max and Carter exchanged another look and both said, "Women's league."

I was still laughing as Max leaned toward Addison and pointed to his cheekbone, probably showing her the remnants of a black eye that I hadn't noticed on the MARTA or in the car.

"And we're there forever," Carter said.

Max nodded. "The games start at eight in the morning, and the last ones end at ten at night. We don't get scheduled for all of them, but they're usually scattered through the day. Carter takes long breaks for lunch and dinner."

"I can't eat indoor soccer field food," Carter complained. "I would starve to death. Max doesn't care. He probably brings his own rabbit food."

"I *do* sometimes bring my own salad," Max said self-righteously. It was pretty weird to sit at a table in the edgy alternative section of Atlanta with two handsome boys who were arguing about salad. Clearly they could argue about *anything*. They were worse than Addison and me.

"If you think I'm underfed," Max said, reaching for a slice of Carter's meat-laden pizza, "you won't mind if I—"

"Nuh nuh nuh nuh," Carter said, thunking Max's knuckle with his finger until Max backed off. Then Carter said, "And Max takes a break to coach his team."

"Oooh, what team do you coach?" Addison asked.

I wanted to know too, but I was afraid to press it. Since Carter had brought it up, he must have thought it would embarrass Max. Max blushed a little, the faintest flush on each cheek in the romantic glow from the strings of lights overhead.

"I coach my little sister's team," Max said.

Carter had miscalculated. Addison and I said, "Awwwwww!" and Addison scooted a little closer to Max.

"How old is she?" Addison asked.

"Ten," Max said.

"Do they wear pink socks over their shin guards," I asked, "and bows in their hair?"

Max grinned. "I have tried to discourage this."

"I'll bet your sister's friends idolize you," I said. "You're like Justin Bieber!"

Addison shrieked laughter, so Max smiled at her rather than me as he admitted, "I am the Justin Bieber of girls' soccer, yes."

"What a boost to your ego," I said.

Carter laughed harder at this than I'd meant him to, then jumped on my comment. "Like that ego needs boosting."

Max looked at Carter. "If my ego were easily boosted—"

"And it is," Carter assured everyone.

"—I would embrace my status as the Biebs of soccer," Max said. "As it is, my sister wanted to play, the league has a hard time recruiting coaches in the summer, and my dad has to work late some nights during the week, when they practice."

"It's probably hard for you, too," I said. What I wanted to say was, *This is the sweetest thing I ever heard, and it is making me fall in love with you,* but I managed to hold back.

He shrugged. "It was fine in June and July. It's hard now that school and football practice have started, but it will be over the weekend of our first football game."

"The weekend Gemma's team will crush us," Carter said.

I stabbed a tomato rather than look at him, because I was afraid the expression on my face would give away how little I liked him at that moment. If Carter was really so concerned about Max being superstitious and losing his mojo for their game, why was he the one bringing it up again? And if he really liked me, why was he going out of his way to embarrass me?

Addison jumped up. "Gemma, come with me to the bathroom."

I arched my eyebrows, by which I meant to convey to her that my mouth was full, and that she was a big girl who could go to the bathroom all by herself.

She did not get the message. She grabbed my arm and hauled me up so fast that I hardly had time to snatch my purse.

In the bathroom she pushed me against the wall and put her hands on her hips. "Are you trying to move in on my date?"

My heart raced. I wasn't trying to move in on Max. I had not thought it was possible. But if I *had* thought it was possible, yeah. I would have been totally busted.

I put on the most perplexed face I could muster as I chewed my tomato very slowly and swallowed. "You mean Max?"

"No, I mean my butt!" she shouted at me. "Stop being

funny, Gemma! He is *my* date, and *I* am the only one who's allowed to be funny."

"I'm not being funny for Max's sake," I reasoned. "I'm being funny and flirting with Carter."

"Carter isn't laughing!" She flounced into a stall and slammed the door.

True enough. I glanced at my watch. The concert would start in half an hour. It would probably last two hours. Driving back to Carter's truck would take thirty minutes, which meant a total of three more hours saddled with this behemoth named Carter. I didn't know how I would get through it if I wasn't even allowed to pretend to be extroverted. It would be torture, sitting there silently while listening to Max crack jokes and not being allowed to respond. I wasn't sure yet how I would get out of it, but I would *not* go on a date with these people again.

I didn't wait for Addison. After a quick coat of lip gloss, I left the restroom and sashayed around the tables, back to the boys. Hunched over in conversation, they didn't notice me coming. I caught the tail end of what Carter was saying: ". . . if she doesn't even know you like her."

This made me a little mad. They were talking about Max liking Addison. Of course she knew. He might not be hanging on her, but he'd asked her out, hadn't he? That was more than anybody had done for *me*.

But I didn't dwell on it, because I'd noticed something else as Carter spoke. Sliding into my seat, I said, "You *are* from Russia! I heard your accent that time."

Carter's expression sent daggers across the table at Max.

Max held up his hands. "This is a secret all of a sudden?"

"It *was* nice to go out with girls from a different school," Carter said acidly, "because they didn't know about that. Just like they didn't know you make girls mad."

"Oh, I think you spilled that in the first five minutes," Max said.

Carter said, "Gemma found out anyway when we walked up here. I'm surprised Addison hasn't slapped you yet."

I glanced at Max across the table, looking so fun and sweet . . . but yeah, the goatee reminded me of his devilish side. I asked him, "Have you gotten slapped before?"

"Yes," he and Carter said in chorus.

"I was twelve, though," Max defended himself.

I could only imagine what a twelve-year-old girl had thought when Max had filleted her psyche and laid it out on a butcher block for her to see. Actually I was intrigued by this and wanted to know more about twelve-year-old Max. This guy had quite a bit of experience not getting along with girls.

But as Addison had reminded me, Max was not my date. I took my curiosity and warm feelings for Max and simply turned my head, directing all that emotion at Carter.

"I like your accent," I said. "It's sexy."

Carter turned to me, too. This shouldn't have been weird, but it was. Usually when he talked to me, he faced straight ahead and made a comment, and I knew from context that his words were meant for me. The most he'd ever bothered to do was tilt his head at me. This time he turned his whole body to face me full-on as he said, "Большое спасибо."

I was so shocked to hear Russian come out of his mouth that I grinned with a lot more emotion than I actually felt. If I *acted* like I felt it, maybe I really *would* feel it. I would start having a better time, and the night would not drag. I could not have Max. Carter *was* handsome. I *was* his date. I would give it a try.

He grinned at me. I slid my hand onto his knee and smiled back. Out of the corner of my eye, I saw Max signal the waiter. He called, "Check, please."

9

I kept up my act during the walk to the concert and the wait to get inside. I touched Carter periodically. That prompted him to say a little more to me, and it was easier for me to think of things to say back to him.

Mrs. Baxter had told the majorette line that the glamour grin was important. We looked better smiling, and we also felt better, as if our bodies assumed there was something to smile about. I had never really felt this way about the majorette grin. It felt like I was gritting my teeth and waiting to drop a baton. But I did feel this way about smiling up at Carter. I made an effort to like him a little better, and then I did.

The concert was easy to get through because it was too loud to talk and too dark to see much. The Dolly Paranoids were chicks who wore leather and beehive hairdos and rocked their guitars, putting on a great show. As long as I watched the stage or glanced over at Max, who clearly was as big a fan as I was, I felt happy to be there. If *this* was what being a teenager was supposed to be like, I had a lot to look forward to.

It was only when the roving spotlight caught Addison that my mood slipped. She frowned at the stage and even sat down in her seat at one point, which nobody else was doing at this show.

Then the spotlight caught Carter. The light glinted in the blond stubble on his chin and danced in his short blond hair. He really was handsome like a model. I only wished he wasn't scowling at the stage—not as if he was bored, like Addison, but as if he *disapproved*.

"Hey," I said to him during a rare slow number. The only way the Dolly Paranoids could perform a love song was to make it ridiculously over the top. I figured Carter didn't recognize that it was a parody of a prom theme rock ballad, not the real thing. I touched his huge hand, looked up at him, and batted my eyelashes, like Addison. "Having fun?"

He glanced down at me with the same scowl he'd given the girls onstage. Then he squinted in the dim light. His features softened. The scowl faded, and nothing was left but a quiet, cute sixteen-year-old boy on a first date, at a concert he hadn't picked, who never knew the right thing to say.

He bent toward me very, very slowly, so I could have turned back to the stage if I'd wanted to, but I didn't want to. He cupped my chin in his hand, and his lips touched mine.

I wasn't sure what to do. I had never kissed a boy before. I had seen it done in movies, though. I had even seen Addison do it.

Mostly I let him lead the way. When Carter's tongue slipped past my lips, I had a moment of panic that I shouldn't let a boy go that far with me. Then I realized I'd gotten that advice in sixth grade. By one week and six days shy of sixteen, an open-mouthed kiss was probably okay.

I showed him my approval by running one hand up his arm to his thick shoulder and behind his neck. I pressed his head closer to mine and stood on tiptoes to reach him. He put both hands around my waist and kissed me harder.

The band reached the climax of their ridiculous faux love song. It would have been easy to imagine that they were making fun of Carter and me. I didn't mind. After quite a few false starts, Carter and I had finally found something we had in common.

The song ended, and the lights brightened for the next

song. Carter let me go, then applauded the band for the first time all night. When the new song started, he put his heavy arm around my shoulders, and I didn't shrug away.

I didn't have to. Addison jerked me out from under him, calling, "Gemma, come with me to the bathroom," as if I had a choice.

Not again. I really did have to pee this time, though, so I let her lead me as she shoved past Max, dragging me after her. I turned around to mouth *sorry* to Max because we'd bumped him, but he wasn't watching us go. He stared up at the stage, not smiling now, with a stubborn set to his jaw that I hadn't seen before.

Even with the restroom door closed, the music echoed, so I had to listen closely and watch Addison's lips as she asked, "Why have you stopped talking? You have got to get Max off me!"

"What do you mean, get him off you?" I hollered back, not even caring that sophisticated college girls reapplying lipstick at the sinks were staring over at us. I thought with alarm that she was saying Max had been pawing her, but I hadn't seen him touch her.

"He is making all these stupid jokes!" she shouted. "He never shuts up!"

"Oh no, that's terrible," I said, one hundred percent confident that the sarcasm would be lost on her. But making fun of her didn't cheer me up. I felt so sad thinking that Max's jokes were wasted on her, spilling on the floor, to be mopped up late tonight after the concert was over, like so many cups of Coke and beer. I wished there was a way I could help her out, poor thing, but I didn't see how.

"And why are you making out with Carter in public?" she yelled. "Everybody is looking at you."

"Well, they certainly are now!" I yelled back. The college girls closed their lipsticks and escaped the bathroom, which had suddenly become a very uncool place to hang out.

I *had* felt self-conscious about kissing Carter during the concert. So I had snuck peeks through half-closed eyelids, and I had not seen anybody paying us any attention whatsoever, except Addison, who had repeatedly looked over at us and poked Max in the side to show him. "Everybody who?" I asked.

"Just everybody!" she exclaimed, exasperated.

"You made out with Jimmy Farmingdale behind the Dairy Queen," I reminded her. "I mean, not just kissed him, but *really* made out with him and let him go down your bra."

"That was *last year*. God!" Now that the other girls had left, Addison stepped up to the mirror and reapplied her own lipstick. "And I can't get Max to touch me."

I folded my arms. "You *want* him to touch you?"

"Well, yeah! If you and Carter can do it, why can't I?"

"I don't know. You were just saying that you wanted me to talk to Max so you wouldn't have to."

"That's talking," she said. "That's different. I would totally make out with him. He is *so hot.*" She pulled down on the middle of her shirt, exposing more of her cleavage.

I stared at her reflection in the mirror until she stuck out her tongue at me and banged into a stall. Was she *trying* to imitate my relationship with Carter? Did she realize kissing Carter was a lot easier for me than talking to him, and now she was throwing that back in my face?

I shook my head. Of course she wasn't. She did not have any insight into what made me tick. That was a completely different friend. Max.

But what she'd said about talking versus kissing made me think, whether she'd meant it to or not. I wasn't sure if I'd been wrong to kiss Carter when I didn't really like him. I needed some guidance. When we went back into the theater, I half expected the band to be playing a song about hypocrisy. It was a song about black-eyed peas and collard greens. I listened very hard, but I could not detect any message at all. Sometimes a country speed-metal song was just a country speed-metal song.

The concert ended then. Max and Addison led the way

back to the car, but he didn't offer her a piggyback ride this time. Carter and I held hands.

Inside the car, the first thing Carter said was, "Turn the radio down, Max, would you?" I wondered whether Carter and I were going to have our own conversation. But the four of us just talked together on the way back to Carter's truck.

I tried to enjoy the drive. All I could think about, though, was Carter's hand on my hand. We weren't sitting close on the wide backseat—we both wore our seat belts, which strapped us to opposite ends—but we were attached there in the middle. If he wanted to hold my hand all the way back, he probably planned to kiss me again once we got to his truck, right? I hadn't minded before. In fact, I'd enjoyed it.

So why did I feel vaguely nauseated at the thought?

Max pulled into the shopping center parking lot and stopped the car next to Carter's truck. It was after hours and the lot had cleared out, so there was nobody to see what Carter and I did next, except Max and Addison.

They bailed out of the car, met in front of it, and laughed about something. I could hear them through the windshield and see her fingers touch a Japanese character on his T-shirt, over his heart.

I looked at Carter. He was watching me. And he would watch me for the rest of the night if I let him, just like he could maintain stony silence for hours on end if I didn't say something. My queasiness grew. So did my frustration.

I unfastened my seat belt, slid across the seat, and kissed him.

He made a soft noise, something between a groan and the word *no*. I paused, wondering if I'd heard wrong. I definitely didn't want to kiss him if he didn't want to kiss me. I must have misheard him, because he put his hands in my hair and kissed me back.

But only for a few seconds. The kiss didn't come to a natural end. He stopped in mid-kiss like he'd suddenly remembered something. He pulled back against the door and looked me in the eye. "Same time next week?"

I had pledged at the restaurant that I would not go out with this group again. I would extricate myself from this strange, silent boy and his gorgeous friend. Addison could find her own way to convince her mother to let her out of the house. People would stop talking about me in band, and I would sink back into the hole I'd crawled out of.

As I looked into Carter's blue eyes, I knew that was not going to happen. My heart was beating ninety to nothing. That had not happened since . . . every conversation I'd had with Max. And before that, majorette tryouts.

I was not willing to let that rush go.

"Yep," I said. "See you next week."

Carter should have given me one last peck on the cheek then, because he liked me and we'd bonded. But he just took off his seat belt and backed out of the car. I got out on my side to move to the front seat for the ride home.

Max and Addison still stood in front of the car. *He* gave *her* a peck on the cheek, and they laughed and parted. Max followed her over to Carter's truck. He patted Carter on the back guy-style, then punched him on the shoulder, hard enough to hurt from the looks of it. Carter glared at him.

Max folded himself into the driver's seat and watched as Carter's truck sped across the empty parking spaces.

We sat there in silence for longer than was comfortable, way longer than was normal for Max. I wondered what he was thinking. He was angry with Carter for something, obviously.

Finally I broke the silence. "The band was amazing."

He turned to me with a grin. "They were, weren't they?"

"Thanks for planning the whole thing. I'm glad we went."

"Me too." He bit his lip. "Addison didn't like them very much."

"Carter didn't either." I paused. "Sometimes I feel like Carter doesn't like *me* very much."

I expected Max to reassure me and tell me I was wrong. Instead, he started the car. We were all the way across the parking lot and turning onto the road before he said, "That didn't seem to matter too much to you when the two of you were going at it."

His eyes met mine. He looked like a stranger now, much older than me, his goatee rugged.

"Going at it?" I croaked.

"You and Carter hardly ever say anything to each other. I can't imagine how you've gotten close. But every time I looked over at you during the concert, or in the backseat, you were letting him put his hands all over you."

"If it bothers you, don't look," I snapped. Then I processed what he'd said. "He had his hands all over me, Max? You're exaggerating a little. We kissed at the concert, and we kissed in the car. Carter was my date. Isn't that what we were supposed to do?"

"That's just it. I don't think you're *supposed* to do any particular thing, but you seem to think so. You think girls let their dates maul them, so that's what you do. Have you ever dated anyone before?"

I glared at him. "Why do you ask? You think bigger girls never date?"

His lips parted, and he glanced over at me before turning his head to the road again. "You're not bigger."

"I *was* bigger."

He settled back in his seat then, relaxing, retreating out of the attack mode he'd been in since Carter and

Addison had left the car. "I asked because you're fifteen years old—"

"Excuse me, Mr. Sixteen, but you're not that much older than me!"

"—and because you're acting like you just got released from a girls-only reform school in Antarctica."

We were on a darker winding road. I puzzled through what he'd said. He had no reason to insult me about kissing Carter unless he was jealous. If he wanted me for himself, he would not go out with Addison instead. Maybe my fantasy had come true, and he'd realized he'd asked out the wrong girl.

Testing this theory, I said, "You have the opposite problem. Addison says you hardly touch her. But that must be because you've dated before, and you have limitless experience. You know how this works." My words came out more bitter than I'd intended. I hadn't meant to attack *him*. I was fishing for information, dying to know why he hadn't made a move on Addison, even when she was wearing that shirt.

I was disappointed when all Max said was, "Exactly." He carefully turned the long car into my driveway.

I hadn't noticed we were so close to home. I didn't want to get out of the car. I wasn't sure where this conversation was going, but I felt like we had something else to say to each other.

He must have felt that way too, because he rolled down his window to let the warm, humid night inside, and turned off the engine.

He scooted his back against the driver's-side door, facing me. The spotlights on the corners of my house slanted weirdly across his smooth face and his goatee. "There's a reason why you and Carter hardly spoke all night, but you were perfectly okay with sucking face with him. I have a theory."

"Oh *no*," I said. This was not how I'd wanted to finish our conversation. "You know how you make girls mad? You're about to do it again. I can feel it."

Max leaned in and looked straight into my eyes. He concentrated on me like he was trying to see into my mind.

My heart raced and my cheeks burned like we were sharing a long look for another reason. Because we were in love.

"You've said Addison didn't want you to lose weight," he said, shattering my little romantic dream. Max was deconstructing me. "Your other friends didn't want you to lose weight either. Even your mom didn't. That means your relationships with all of them were affected by what you looked like. If you lost weight, your relationships would change, and you knew it."

He paused. Maybe it was just that my eyes had adjusted

to the spotlight on my house shining into the car, but Max's face seemed harsher than before, the lines more angular. This time I looked away.

"Sure enough," he said, "you and Addison are at each other's throats, in your own quiet way. Neither of you verbalizes it, but I can feel the tension coming off the two of you. Your friendship is hard now. Before, it might not have been good, but it was easy. All your relationships were easy. You knew your place with everybody. And that was important to you."

A shadow flitted across the spotlight beam. Bats were dipping in and out of the light.

"Maybe you worked very hard at a relationship," he said quietly, "and it crumbled, despite everything you tried. How long has it been since you saw your dad?"

It felt like my heart was beating somewhere down in my gut. I said weakly, "I've told you. He lives in Hilton Head and runs all these businesses, so it's hard for him to come all the way over here just to see me."

Max didn't say anything. He could have changed the subject with a joke and made me feel better. But he was content to open a wound and then just sit there and watch it bleed.

I asked angrily, "What are you planning for your college major? Psychology?"

His dark brows knitted. "No. My dad wants me to go to Tech and major in engineering. He says psychologists don't make enough money."

"And why don't you tell him what you really want to do?" I sneered. "Because that would make your relationship hard?"

"I like reading people," he said. "I think I'm good at it. That doesn't mean I'm good at reading myself, or solving my own problems."

"Obviously," I said, "because you just caused another problem. You're right. I don't like complicated relationships. You know what's really complicated? Being friends with my best friend's date. So don't think you have to pick me up anymore. You're smart enough to arrange another way to go out with Addison." I opened the door.

"Gemma," he said. His hand squeezed my thigh. Electricity shot across my skin, up my torso, and across my chest to my heart, which pounded like I'd just finished a workout.

I slid out from under his touch and slammed the door behind me.

10

As I stomped across the yard, I realized I shouldn't have slammed Max's door. My mother might have heard it. She might be watching me out a window now. She would know from the way I walked that I was angry. She would hear that anger again if I slammed the front door behind me. Then we'd have to talk about what had happened.

I'd thought I longed to have the chat with her that she kept promising me. But the prospect of talking to her about something this real made me cringe. I didn't want her to know I had a complicated relationship with Max. Then I would have a more complicated relationship with *her*. Max was right, and that made me even madder at him.

I closed the front door, careful to shut it the way I normally did, which I probably got completely wrong now that I was thinking so hard about it.

Then I edged to the window to peek out at the driveway. I half expected—or half hoped—Max would still be parked there, staring mournfully at my house, contemplating running after me and ringing the (oh God) gong doorbell to tell me he was sorry. But he was already backing into the street, probably not even thinking about my prissy little fit.

I watched him until his taillights disappeared around the corner.

In the kitchen, I peered into the refrigerator, then the freezer, then the refrigerator again, looking for . . . something. I asked myself whether I was hungry or just wanted something to eat. The answer was neither. I wanted Max to come back. I wanted to erase what I had said, and what he had said, and go back to a time before I saw myself so clearly. I didn't like what I saw.

I climbed the stairs. My mom was in her office. Really I thought of it as Dad's office, though it had been Mom's for the past six years. She hadn't redecorated after Dad left. The walls were still painted a manly forest green and lined with towering dark wood cabinets. She seemed out of place in Dad's leather office chair, sitting behind his massive wooden desk and pecking at the computer. A bowl and a spoon sat next to the keyboard. Without looking, I knew the bowl had held cobbler and ice cream, and that it was empty.

When I stood in the doorway, she didn't glance up from hunting and pecking. My high school made everybody take typing now, but she had missed out on that. And apparently, working for a few years as a secretary before marrying my dad had not taught her any keyboarding skills. Biting her lip, she was really intent on finding that *G* or whatever.

"Hi, Mom," I finally said. "I'm back."

"Oh, hey, sweetie." She pecked another letter before she looked up. Her brow furrowed. "What's the matter? Didn't you have fun on your date with Max?"

"Sure," I lied. Wait. "Carter. My date with Carter."

"That's what I said." She went back to typing. Over the clicks of the keyboard, she called, "Let me finish this up, and then I want to hear all about it."

Right. I knew how it worked. We wouldn't talk again until morning, when she would make me a big breakfast and I'd refuse to eat it.

I wandered down the hall to my room and sank down

on my bed, thinking hard about Max. I had lashed out at him instinctively because what he'd said had hurt—like slapping a mosquito when it stung me.

But he had been right about a lot. He was so right about my "friendship" with Addison that I almost felt like I should apologize to her for losing weight and making the majorette line. I'd gained confidence, I'd started fighting for my own friendships with people, and I'd ruined the nice, peaceful princess-and-servant relationship that Addison and I had had before.

I *knew* I should apologize to Max for getting so angry. And telling him I couldn't be friends with him anymore. What if he took that *seriously*?

I pulled my phone from my purse. With a shaking finger, I flipped to his number and called him.

"Hello?" he said.

I'd never heard him over the phone before. His low voice sent a shiver through the center of my chest.

"It's Gemma." He should have known it was me, since he had my number in his phone, but he didn't sound like he knew who was calling.

"Hi, Gemma," he said evenly.

"I'm sorry about what I said to you," I blurted. "I didn't mean it. I guess I got really mad at you for understanding so much about me. You got a little too close for comfort.

Like you said, knowing what your problems are doesn't always help you solve them, and I—"

"Gemma," he interrupted me. "I do want to hear this story, but can we talk about it later? I'm on the phone with Addison."

I was so surprised that I let the silence stretch way too long.

I'd thought our relationship was important to him, but I was just his date's friend after all.

"No, that's fine," I said. "I'll see you later."

"Okay. See ya." He hung up.

I stared at my phone until my vision blurred with tears. Then I lay back on the bed and stared at the blurry lines of beadboard in the ornate dropped ceiling. I was so tired. I just wanted to sleep and forget it all.

But I hadn't practiced baton yet, except during band period at school. I'd taught fourth graders at the baton studio, but I was just showing them simple stuff like vertical spins. If I wasn't perfecting my illusions, which I loved to do now that my thighs had shrunk, I didn't feel like I'd practiced at all.

I snuck down into the dark yard, intending to practice only until midnight. But the more I tried not to think about Max, the angrier I got, and the faster I twirled. I stayed out until one.

* * *

All week at school, I worried about my upcoming date with Carter and Addison's date with Max. People I vaguely knew continued to stop me in the hall and ask me in a friendly way if I was really dating the quarterback from East. One day during band practice, Delilah even whispered that she'd heard I'd made out with him—was that true? The only possible source of this rumor was Addison. And since Delilah managed to make everything sound like a compliment, I couldn't tell whether Addison had spread this information to help me or hurt me.

Though I could take a guess. The vote for head majorette–elect was coming up in less than two weeks. If rumors were circulating about me, then Mrs. Baxter would think I wasn't keeping my nose clean.

On Friday I still hadn't heard the plan for our date that night. During a lull in band practice, when the director stood way up in the stands and made minute adjustments to the trombones standing in a curlicue on the football field, I slipped my phone from my pocket and checked my messages. Nothing. The idea of Carter calling me made my stomach go south, but I wanted to know whether we still had a date. More importantly, I wanted to know whether I would ever see Max again.

Addison walked over from her place on the thirty-five

yard line to my place on the forty and plopped down beside me in the grass. "Ready for tonight? It sounds like a bore to me."

I was loath to admit she knew something I didn't, but that had been the case all along with us and these boys. "I haven't talked to Carter," I said. "Where are we going?"

She raised her eyebrows in surprise. "We're seeing some kung fu movie at the Fox and getting coffee after. We need to hint that Carter should start coming up with these dates, not Max."

I suppressed a laugh. The Fox was a gorgeous 1920s theater not far from where we lived. When it wasn't hosting concerts or plays, it showed classic movies. Trust Max to find the most offbeat movie they showed. It sounded like a blast to me.

If Carter planned our date? Wow, it sounded like a chain restaurant and a blockbuster movie to me. What a yawn. Addison would love it.

"So Max called you?" I asked. "That's great, right?"

She shook her head. "No, I got a text from Carter today."

"But Max called you earlier in the week, right?"

"No, why?"

"Oh. I just figured he would, since he kissed you after the concert," I said casually, even though my heart was pounding. Max had lied to me Friday night when he said he was on the phone with Addison. He'd been trying to make me jealous. Which must mean he liked me!

After that initial spike of adrenaline, though, I talked myself down off the ledge. He could have been trying to make me jealous, or more likely, he was angry that I'd *yelled at him*. He'd probably been mad and hadn't wanted to talk to me when I'd called to apologize.

That was all.

"It was the lamest kiss ever," Addison was saying. "I get a sexier kiss than that from my grandpa."

Despite the fact that I'd talked myself out of thinking Max liked me, it made me happy that their kiss had been no big deal. If she hadn't gotten into it, maybe he hadn't either.

"But you"—she tapped my cell phone on my knee—"have been getting calls from Carter, right?"

"No." I tried not to sound relieved about that. "Why?"

"Because it's totally rude of him to ignore you after the way y'all were swapping slobber last Friday."

She watched me to see if I reacted. I gave her my majorette grin. The very idea that she was spreading rumors about Carter and me made my stomach hurt. But if I let her see that, she would know what bothered me, and she would do more of it.

Standing up and brushing the grass off her butt, she

said, "I'm gonna go talk to Susan," without even trying to disguise that talking to me bored her. Susan was the head majorette. Addison made the rounds every day, ingratiating herself to all the majorettes so she could get their votes for head-elect. She was wasting a lot of energy if you asked me. There was no way I would be chosen, and Delilah only had a chance if she stopped turning ashen every time the band started the opening number.

Robert plopped down beside me the instant Addison stepped away, as if he'd been hovering, waiting for his opportunity. "Hey, Gemma." With a giant nod, he gave his dyed-black hair a toss out of his eyes.

I just stared at him for a moment. He had a lot of nerve trying to share my forty yard line without asking. "Hey," I said warily.

"Want to go out tonight?"

I had waited two whole years to hear those words, and Robert asked nonchalantly, like he was asking to borrow a dollar.

I wasn't happy about the prospect of another night tolerating Carter and pining for Max, but it sure was nice to be able to tell Robert I had other things to do. "I have plans."

"With that quarterback?" he asked. "I heard about that. But y'all aren't serious, are you? How about tomorrow night?"

I hardly dared to ask, because he might make fun of me, but I needed to know. "Robert, are you asking me out on a date?"

He spread his hands. "Duh! What did you think?"

I was quiet. I wanted to shout, *What I* thought *was, you sent me a sympathy card right before majorette tryouts last April.* But I didn't.

Then I remembered Max saying I only wanted relationships that weren't complicated. If I told Robert how I felt right now, things would get complicated.

And so I told him. "What I *thought* was, you sent me a sympathy card right before majorette tryouts last April."

"That was a joke!" he exclaimed. "We always used to send each other cards like that."

"No, not like that, Robert," I told him sternly. "Not sympathy cards. Not before an important tryout. You shouldn't have done that. A good friend wouldn't do that. Then you sent me a text message that I'd sold out. And *then* you stopped speaking to me."

He pointed at me. "*You* stopped speaking to *me.* The day after you made majorette, you sicced Delilah Allen on me in history class."

"I did not *sic* her on you," I said, almost laughing at the thought of tiny Delilah scaring the bejesus out of a full-grown guy. "I told her about the card. She must have taken it upon herself to tell you what she thought of how you treated your so-called friend."

Robert furrowed his brow and shook his head like this did not compute. "You stopped talking to *all* of us, not just me. You lost weight, you made majorette, and you became a different person."

He was wrong. I had been very careful *not* to become a different person. And I wasn't going to let him off the hook. "You wouldn't know whether I became a different person or not," I pointed out, "because you stopped speaking to me."

He blinked at me in surprise, then tossed his hair out of his eyes again to give himself time to think. He had never seen this Gemma before, Gemma Who Bites Back.

He put his hand on my hand. "I miss you," he said quietly. "I think up these jokes that nobody would get but you, and I don't have anyone to tell them to."

I looked into his big gray eyes. I missed him, too. I missed his jokes. He was funny—very funny. He was a lot like Max, except that Max was even quicker, and a whole lot cuter, and bore no malice.

Usually.

And Robert was right. Just because Carter and I had been on a date and had planned another did not mean we were dating exclusively. I could go out with Carter tonight and Robert tomorrow. Then the school would *really* talk about me. I would be That Majorette Who Dates a Lot. I took a breath to tell Robert yes.

But my stomach twisted at the thought of going out with Robert, just as it twisted at the thought of going out with Carter again. What was I doing, exactly? Aiming for quantity, not quality?

My cell phone vibrated with a text message. I started and pulled my hand away from Robert. The text was from Max. With a sidelong glance at Robert, I read it.

7:30 tonight? No more of my theories, promise.

I bit my lip to keep from laughing. Driving to the theater with Max sounded a lot more fun than a date with Robert and a date with Carter combined. I might not ever have Max, but I could do better than Robert.

I texted Max—**See u then**—and clicked my phone off. "Robert, you've told me before that you just wanted to be friends. I think that's best for us." I didn't give him time for a bitter comeback. I plowed ahead, "But I miss you, too. We could go out as friends. I have a lot to tell you. I went to see the Dolly Paranoids last week."

"You did?" Surprise and admiration overtook the defensiveness in his voice, at least for a moment.

The band director called through the megaphone, telling us to return to our places and run the drill again. I stood, pocketed my phone, and picked up my batons. I spent the rest of the period lost in twirling my batons and my own swirling thoughts, proud of myself for standing up to Robert and wishing seven thirty would come right now.

I was worried about what I would wear, though. I knew I had no chance with Max, but I still didn't want him to see me in my MARCHING WILDCATS T-shirt again. Addison had thrown down the gauntlet with her boob-baring blouse last Friday. I wasn't going down without a fight.

As the debutante ball approached, Addison had more meetings to attend after school. Lately my mom picked me up. I could ask her to take me to my favorite vintage clothing store, which I hadn't visited since I'd started losing weight. She didn't understand why I wanted to wear used clothes, but she didn't want to argue with me about it either. She would sit in the car and wait for me, as usual.

As I made this plan, I felt a pang of loneliness. I wished I had a girlfriend to go shopping with. I longed for last year when Addison had been available to shop with me. But as the majorette line turned left for a high toss and I watched her drop her baton, I realized I didn't miss her. She would turn up her nose at every top I picked out. I wished for company, but she was not the one that I wanted.

The majorette line faced right for another high toss, which Delilah caught expertly. I couldn't see her face, but I knew her grin was confident while the stadium was almost empty. We saw each other every school day, but I hadn't checked in with her lately about our first performance next week and her battle against stage fright. I would have loved to ask *her* to take me shopping that afternoon. We would get a chance to talk one-on-one. I couldn't suggest it, though, because Addison would get jealous and act pissed off.

With one more turn to the left, gazing at Addison's back, I decided I was not going to let her petty jealousies control me. As I'd told her at majorette tryouts, I could have more than one friend. On the way out of band practice, I would ask Delilah to go shopping with me.

My girlfriend life was going to get as complicated as my boyfriend life.

So be it.

"None of that is going to fit you," Delilah advised me as I pushed through the curtain, into the fitting room, with an armload of clothes.

I had my doubts too. When we'd first arrived, the sales chicks had gawked and squealed over me because I looked so different. They had always set aside cool pieces for me in bigger sizes, but this time they'd warned me these would be too big for me. They'd said the store was full of clothes that would fit me better.

Obediently I'd browsed the regular racks and found the coolest pink bowling shirt with the name GLADYS embroidered in cursive on the pocket—exactly the top I'd been hoping to find. Max would laugh out loud when he saw it. It looked tiny, though. I'd put it back.

But as I reached up to hang the clothes on the hook, I found the bowling shirt, like it was following me. There was also a top I hadn't seen before: white, one-shouldered, printed with 1960s satellites, and sewn with sequins. It was the weirdest thing I had ever seen. I loved it. I would never have chosen it for myself because it looked too small. Also, my boobs were too big for a strapless bra to corral—at least, they *had* been.

"Did you pick out this bowling shirt and this one-shouldered white blouse?" I called over the wall to Delilah in the next fitting room. "Did you mean to put them in your pile?" This didn't seem likely. Delilah was a flowery type, like the gorgeous trapeze dress I'd found for her. She was not a satellite type or a bowling shirt type.

"Of course I meant them for you," came her voice through the wall. "They look *just like you*. Did you try them on? They're my size, and I think we're about the same."

Considering her petite frame, I found this hard to

believe. But out of curiosity, I slipped the one-shouldered top over my head. It was silky against my skin. And it fit. It pooled at my neckline, showing just a hint of cleavage. And then, of course, there were the satellites. If any shirt was going to catch Max's attention, this would be it.

As I examined myself in the mirror and turned a little to let the sequins reflect the light, I felt a wave of déjà vu. I'd been in this dressing room a million times. I'd slipped into shirts and gazed at myself critically in the mirror. I'd gone for loud retro fashions because they told the world I wasn't afraid to be noticed. I was big, I was comfortable with my body, and I did not care what people thought of me. That wasn't true, of course—I *wasn't* comfortable and I *did* care—but I didn't want to admit it.

Suddenly depressed, I collapsed on the velvet settee in the corner, inhaling the slightly mildewed scent of the shop. In a much smaller retro top printed with satellites, I still cared what people thought of me. And it was still important to me to tell them I didn't. Robert had asked me out, my dream come true, and I had moved on to fantasizing about a new guy I couldn't have. I might have lost weight and made majorette, but nothing else had changed. I was back where I started.

"Are you ready for the big reveal?" Delilah called.

"Sure." I hopped up from the velvet seat and raked open

the lacy curtain. "Wow!" I exclaimed. "You look so classic!" I turned her around so we both looked down the hall at the three-way mirror. "And for something different, you could belt this." I put my hands on either side of her waist in the flowered dress. "You could wear a scarf around your neck. I hope you're buying it! Was I right or was I right?"

"You were right," she acknowledged. "But wow yourself! That top is so you, and you look *hot*. Is this for your date tonight?"

"Definitely," I said, grinning into the mirror.

"I can tell you really like him," she said.

I watched my grin fade and my bare shoulder sag. "Sometimes two people are meant to be together," I said. "We're not."

"Really?" she asked, peering at me with her brow knitted. "I could have sworn, the way you were acting—"

I interrupted her before she could draw out my feelings for Max. She thought we were talking about Carter. I didn't mind talking about him at all. "Every date doesn't have to be with The One, right? I can still go out with him and have fun." Fun with Max, that is.

"Sure you can," she said, but the perplexed expression stayed in her eyes. She knew I was leaving something out.

I changed the subject. "What about you? Are you dating? You never talk about it."

"Oh, no." She shook her head. "You know how I get so worked up about baton performances? I act the same way around guys."

"Guys make you faint?" I joked. Then I wished I hadn't made the joke. It seemed that was exactly what she was saying.

"No!" She waved one hand as if this idea was ridiculous. "I never get that far. I just stay away from them."

"I talked to Robert during band practice. He said you really laid into him about sending me that sympathy card before tryouts last April."

She put her hand over her mouth. "Are you mad?"

"Of course I'm not mad! Just surprised. And it doesn't sound like guys make you nervous."

"When he sent you that card, it pissed me off!" she squeaked. "I'd watched the two of you laughing together. You lit up when you were around him, and he was so cute, doing that thing with his hair." She jerked her head in her perfect imitation of Robert tossing the hair out of his eyes. "I was a little jealous, honestly, that you could talk to each other for hours like that. But he was always going out with some other girl he didn't talk to! I thought it was a matter of time until you got together as a couple. I couldn't *believe* he sent you that card, like he was *trying* to ruin your friendship."

As I nodded, I glanced at myself in the mirror again. I was surprised at how grim I looked, lips pressed into a straight line. "He asked me out today."

Delilah lit up. "He did?" she exclaimed. "Finally, Gemma! That is so great! Did you say yes?"

I shook my head.

She bit her lip. "Because of the card?"

"The card, and a lot of things," I said. "Too much water has gone under that bridge."

"He should have known better than to treat you that way. Maybe he learned his lesson." She wrapped her arm around my waist. We gazed at ourselves in our decades-old clothes that fit us so well. "You look gorgeous, Gemma. You're going to have so much fun on your date tonight. Go ahead and tell me this guy isn't right for you. Maybe you even believe that yourself. But your heart is showing on your sleeve." She rubbed my bare arm. "I don't believe it for a second."

11

"Cool shirt," Max said.

"Thanks!" I exclaimed.

I had started getting ready for the date in plenty of time, I'd thought. But the top was so figure-flattering that I'd felt self-conscious about how the rest of me looked. I'd put my hair up, then down, and up, then down again. By the time I'd finally settled on a look, it was seven thirty. I wasn't waiting outside when Max arrived, so he'd rung the gong doorbell.

I wasn't sure whether he'd complimented my shirt to put me at ease while the stupid gong echoed in the marble entryway, or because he actually thought the shirt was cool. I was grateful to him regardless.

"It's like the space race meets Studio 54," he said.

"I thought you'd like it." I hadn't meant to say that out loud. I felt my face turn red.

I must have embarrassed him, too, because he asked quickly, "Do I look foreign in this?"

"Hmm." I considered him. The goatee was gone. His chin and cheeks were smooth again. It was *so weird* to think about him as much as I did all week, but to have no idea what he looked like from day to day. He was out living his life, and I was missing the whole thing.

I forced my eyes away from his face and examined him from head to toe, concluding, "Yes, you look foreign."

"But it's not the shirt, right? My shirt is in English."

"It's the necklace," I said.

He fingered the round gold charm on a red cord. The cord was too tight for him to see the charm well. He tried to peer down at it with one eye closed. He looked adorable when he did this, and I wanted to kick myself for thinking so.

"And the shoes," I said.

He held out a foot and looked at his sneaker. "What's wrong with my shoes?"

"I've never seen that brand before. They don't necessarily look Japanese. They might be German. Definitely foreign."

"I bought them in New York."

"In Atlanta, that's foreign."

"Touché." He grinned at me.

I wondered whether he was making a joke about Addison's comment from our dinner at the Varsity: *Tissue? Tush?* I didn't ask because I had promised myself I wouldn't dis Addison in front of him. He had promised not to present me with any more of his theories about my subconscious. With our usual subject matter off-limits, we laughed and talked about local bands all the way to the Fox without really saying a thing.

He was able to find a parking space pretty close to the theater. Bruce Lee was not a big draw at the Fox, apparently. Carter and Addison were waiting for us out front. Addison was wearing a minidress that was so tight I doubted she could breathe. My space-race-meets-Studio-54 top could not compete with her minidress. I had lost again. But this hardly registered, because I was so nervous about greeting Carter.

"Hey, Gemma," he said, putting one hand on my waist and the other behind my bare shoulder, pulling me close. Before I could back away or yell*, Fire!* he kissed me on the mouth. He deepened the kiss, and I froze. I didn't like being stared at on the busy sidewalk.

He finally broke away. The blinking neon lights of the

theater facade flickered green across his face. He didn't look apologetic or embarrassed. He looked triumphant, like he'd just won a game. Then he glanced over at Max.

Max stood at the ticket window, with Addison beside him. Their backs were toward us.

Nope, I wasn't going to worry about it. I was through puzzling these boys out. Carter wanted to date me or he wouldn't have asked. When he didn't want to date me anymore, he would stop asking. I was just glad to be on a date with a handsome boy, at this beautiful theater, seeing an offbeat movie. And I was glad the show would start soon. Carter and I would have almost no dead space to fill with awkward conversation.

My luck got even better. Carter and I would have *no* dead space to fill. As soon as we all pushed through the outer door into the plush theater lobby, Addison grabbed me and said, "Gemma, come with me to the bathroom."

At least, I'd *thought* this was great luck. I'd forgotten that Addison always had something choice to say when she dragged me to the bathroom and pushed me against the wall. This time it was the following:

"Stop paying your own way! It makes me look bad!" She turned to the mirror and ran her fingers underneath her eyes, smoothing her eyeliner, as if what she'd said should make perfect sense to me.

"I beg your pardon?"

She whirled to face me. "Don't play dumb. You paid for your movie ticket. You paid for your concert ticket last week. You even paid for your *salad* or whatever the hell you ate at the *pizza* place. If you pay your own way, you make it look like *I* should pay *my* own way."

"Why shouldn't you?" I asked. "Max is paying his way *and* your way out of his referee money, I'm sure. That's why I pay my way. I have my own money from teaching at the baton studio. Carter shouldn't have to spend his referee money on me."

"I don't have a job!" she flung at me before stomping into a stall.

I stood facing the stall door. I had never been to summer camp because there were all these urban legends about mean girls putting hair remover in each other's shampoo. I could not imagine someone being that evil, but I was absolutely certain that if this evil girl existed, she would be placed in my cabin, I would be her target, and I would go bald.

Suddenly I understood that evil girl. I wanted very badly to put hair remover in Addison's shampoo.

Again, I remembered what Max had told me the week before. I avoided conflict so my relationships would not get complicated. But now was not the time to tell Addison how I felt. I wanted to damage her, and that might get me arrested.

I gritted my teeth and turned on my majorette grin, but it didn't make me feel any happier. I walked back out to the boys, who were waiting for us in the lobby. I was glad that they were engrossed in conversation about kung fu movies. I could just listen to them and watch Max laugh without participating myself.

Carter draped his heavy arm around my shoulders. After a few minutes, when Addison emerged from the restroom, we went to take our seats. Carter kept his arm around me and steered me into the theater. As we sat down, he held my hand and didn't let it go.

When Bruce Lee started making out with his on-screen lady, Carter leaned over and kissed me. I couldn't will myself to enjoy it this time. As his tongue moved inside my mouth, Max's voice was in the back of my head: *Every time I looked over at you, he had his hands all over you, and you were letting him.* And Max was right. I was tired of pretending to like Carter.

Carter broke the kiss and sat up straight. Beyond Carter's broad body, Max stared at me with a scowl on his face. He turned back to the movie screen and didn't look at me again. I was so preoccupied by what Max's scowl had meant that I couldn't focus on the rest of the movie.

Carter held my hand again as we walked out of the theater and down the street to a coffee shop. Ignoring the look Addison gave me, I ordered and paid for my own iced coffee. We all sat at a booth in the front of the shop overlooking the sidewalk. Carter put his arm around my shoulders *again*.

"How's football practice going?" Addison asked. She sipped at the smoothie Max had bought her. Either she hadn't figured out that football was a touchy subject for these boys, or she thought the drama would be entertaining.

"Max wouldn't know," Carter said.

Max rolled his eyes.

Addison turned to Max. "Have you been out sick?"

"No, he's been at practice," Carter said. "But he's not really part of the team."

"How can you say that?" I leaned away from Carter so that I could look at him—and slide out from under his arm. "The kicker is responsible for half the points in a lot of games."

"Not in ours, he won't be," Carter said proudly.

I expected Max to have a witty comeback. But his shoulders sagged, and he looked out the window. He'd heard this verbal abuse so often that it didn't even touch him anymore—or he was just waiting for it to be over.

Like with Addison and me.

I had had enough. "You're saying most of your points are going to be touchdowns?" I asked Carter. "That's a pretty big boast. If your running game falls apart, Max will be right there, waiting to save the game for you. That's what the kicker is *for*. I still don't see why you talk like he's not part of the team."

"He isn't," Carter insisted. "You think you know everything about football, Gemma, but you haven't been to practice. We're doing tackle drills the whole time. Hell, I'm the quarterback and *I'm* doing tackle drills. And where's Max? Off on the sidelines, kicking, like he's too good to practice with the rest of us."

"But isn't that what he's *supposed* to be doing?" I asked. "Isn't that what the coach is *telling* him to do?"

Max turned to Carter and raised his eyebrows in question.

"Maybe so," Carter said, "but the coach doesn't tell him to have this pretty boy, holier-than-thou attitude."

Carter scowled, which made his whole face look twisted. His words were illogical, but the emotion behind them was very real. I knew he and Max had been friends forever. A little part of him hated Max for something. I doubted that something was Max being a kicker. Judging from my own relationship with Addison, I guessed the source of this argument was really jealousy over a prize Hot Wheels set when they were nine, or some mortifying slight one had committed against the other in front of a group of girls when they were twelve.

The longer I stared at him, the uglier Carter looked. He still was model-handsome in that giant I-could-crush-you-with-my-pinkie way, but the look on his face revolted me.

Because I recognized that scowl. I had seen it in my reflection whenever I caught a glimpse of myself in the glass doors while practicing my baton routines in my backyard, driven by anger at Addison.

Max leaned across the table toward Carter. His expression was earnest. "I don't feel like I have that attitude at all. I feel like I'm the only Japanese guy on the team. The other guys think I'm an outsider. And when you tell people I'm a pretty boy, you're not helping."

"You're the only Japanese guy on your team?" Addison asked. "There are lots of Japanese kids at our school."

I opened my mouth to say something, anything, to draw her into a conversation so she wouldn't interrupt Max again. This was a talk Max and Carter needed to have.

But Max had already turned on her. "By 'lots,' do you mean three? They're probably Chinese or Korean. There are more of them in Atlanta than Japanese."

Addison shrugged. "What's the difference?"

Carter and I gaped at Addison, both of us horrified at what she'd said and afraid of what Max would do.

Before Max could say anything, I put my hand on his and said soothingly, "She didn't mean it that way, Max—"

He balled his hand into a fist and leaned toward Addison. "What's the difference between Japan and China?" he asked sarcastically and too loudly for this coffee shop full of college-age kids and adults. "A language. An entire culture."

"Max," Carter said sharply to snap him out of it.

"Two thousand seven hundred years of history!" Max sneered down at Addison, who backed against the window and cringed.

"Come on." I jumped up from the booth and grabbed Max's elbow. I hauled him toward the door, motioning to Carter to keep Addison there. Carter nodded. Shaken, Addison put her head down on the table, and Carter stroked her hair. I thought that was strange. I'd never seen Addison and Carter touch before.

But I was more concerned about Max. My heart pounded in my chest as I dragged him out to the sidewalk, away from the windows where Addison and Carter could watch us. I led him around the corner of the brick building and stopped him. The sidewalks were filled with yuppies having date night, so I kept my voice low as I said, "Maybe you shouldn't have caffeine this late. Addison didn't deserve to get yelled at."

"She did!" he snapped. He was still wound up. I saw in his eyes that I was getting the full force of his anger.

I made my voice soothing, but I didn't pull any punches. "You brought it up, Max," I reminded him. "You talked about being Japanese on your team. You didn't have to say that in front of her. You baited her in the first place. You confused her by taking her to a Chinese movie with Japanese bad guys. If you're sensitive about a topic, don't bring up the topic." Not around Addison, anyway. "I don't go around talking about losing weight, do I?"

"I'm not *sensitive* about being *Asian*," he insisted. "It's an entire race. Half the population of the planet is Asian. I can't be sensitive about that. I'm not sensitive about being a man, either, or having two ears. I should be able to talk about the basic facts of who I am without being insulted."

I put my hand on his chest, over his racing heart. "As you have pointed out, Asians aren't the majority in Atlanta, or even a large minority. She hasn't been exposed much to those cultures. All she meant was that she doesn't know the difference. She wasn't trying to make fun of you or belittle you."

Exasperated, he ran one hand through his hair.

"Enough people do, though, right? Make fun of you and

belittle you? I know the feeling. But not every conversation is an attack. You don't need to accuse somebody of lashing out at you when they're not. Don't take your anger at Carter out on Addison."

Max frowned—something he did not do often. He started, "What do you—"

"You know what I mean," I interrupted. "*Why* is Carter on your case about kicking? He's the quarterback, and he acts like he's never heard of your position. There's something else going on between you, isn't there?"

"Yeah. It's kind of hard to explain."

"Try. It's getting weird, and I'm getting tired of teaching Carter football."

Max chuckled, but there was no humor in the sound. "Well, Carter didn't speak English all that well when he came to America, so he got behind in school. He's always had trouble making friends, for the same reason. The first sport we played together was soccer, but being a big guy isn't an advantage there. It's an advantage in football, and when we started playing, he was a lot better than me."

I nodded. "And then you became a kicker."

"Yeah." Max sighed—because he was worried about the situation with Carter. Or because he was relieved I understood what he was explaining to me. I couldn't tell.

"Carter's a great quarterback, but you're a great kicker,"

I said, piecing it together. "He finally found one thing he was better at than you, and now he's lost that."

Max shrugged. "I mean . . . I'm not even sure that's what he's mad about. That's what I think, but I don't know."

"Why don't you ask him?"

Max laughed, and this time his heart was in it. "Have a conversation with my friend about how we really feel? *You're* one to make that suggestion."

"*I* don't communicate very well with my friends," I acknowledged, "but *you* do."

"With you," he said. "Not with guys. Guys would think I couldn't take the pressure." He rubbed his eyes with one hand, then held his head, eyes squinted shut. "How could Addison make a mistake like that? You go to the same high school, with its three Chinese or whoever they are, and *you've* never made a mistake like that."

"Jesus, Max, would you let it go? I make plenty of mistakes. I ruined your mojo, remember?"

He put down his hand and stared at me with wide, serious eyes. "Don't say that."

"And *you* make mistakes. I don't know what they are, but I'm sure you've made one before."

My hand was still on his chest. His heartbeat had slowed as we talked. Now I felt it speed up beneath my fingertips.

He swallowed and said softly, "I sure have."

Oh God. Max was trying to tell me that he wished he'd asked me out instead of Addison!

Or, was he? As he watched me with his long lashes blinking slowly over his dark eyes, I began to wonder. Maybe he wished he'd never met either of us. If he broke up with Addison, that would be the end of *my* friendship with Max too.

"What do you mean by that?" I asked. It came out a whisper.

"Nothing," he grumbled, walking away. My hand slipped off his chest.

I wanted to pull him back, to tell him to wait. But I was beginning to feel like a puppy following him around and barking at his heels. So I hung back a few paces as he strode around the corner and up the sidewalk toward Addison. I wanted to plead with him not to break up with her forever, but all I could do was hold my breath.

By the time I reached the booth, he'd slid next to Addison and was talking earnestly to her, holding her hand. She looked upset, but her eyes were dry.

As I approached, Max stood up, pulling Addison with him. He frowned at Carter and said, "We're going to my car. Give me five minutes." His scowl sent the message, *Or else*. As they left the shop, he didn't glance at me.

I slid into the seat they'd vacated and reached across the table for my iced coffee. The ice had melted.

Carter looked at his watch, marking the beginning of the five-minute period. Go.

I sipped my coffee. "You shouldn't have called Max a pretty boy."

"You don't know. You're not there." Carter stared down at the table. "It's my team."

"It's not your team. It's Max's team too."

We didn't say another word for the rest of the five minutes. He signaled that time was up by standing.

Outside, I led the way to where Max had parked. We emerged from a tree-lined section of the sidewalk to see Max and Addison kissing in the front seat of his car. Not making out, exactly, but not a peck on the cheek, either. His mouth was on her mouth. His hand cupped her jaw.

My stomach sank. So he was glad to be with her after all. And the mistake he told me he'd made was . . . getting close to *me*?

Which meant that I hadn't been imagining things. He *had* liked me.

And somehow I had blown it.

I looked up at Carter. "Good night."

"Good night," he said, hardly glancing at me. He stared at Max and Addison.

They parted and opened their eyes. Max glanced at us through the back window. They exchanged what must have been one last whispered declaration of love, and Addison scooted out of the passenger side and walked up the sidewalk to Carter. "I'll call you," she lied to me.

Carter and Max didn't even wave to each other.

I shuffled down the sidewalk, climbed through the door Addison had left open, and closed it behind me. I faced forward, watching in the side mirror as Addison and Carter hike slowly back up the street.

Max started the car and pulled into traffic.

The silence was excruciating. Even the radio was off.

He finally broke the silence when he turned the car into my neighborhood. "We should plan something really special for your birthday next Thursday. We can go out then, since we all have the game on Friday." His words were sweet, but he enunciated them with fake emotion, like he was reading off a cue card.

"Yes," I said in the same tone. "That—sounds—like—fun!"

He glared at me across the car. "Why are you so mad?"

"I'm not mad."

"You've been mad since I kissed Addison." He sounded proud of himself. When I looked over, I caught a glimpse of the smug expression on his face before he could wipe it off.

"I have not been mad at you," I said haughtily. "You're *supposed* to kiss a girl when you're on a date with her."

"So you're relieved that I'm finally kissing your friend," he prompted me.

Now I was exasperated. "Yes! Sure. I'm totally monitoring your love life, Max. The two of you have such great chemistry. I know this relationship is going to last forever."

He pulled into my driveway. As soon as the car stopped, I got out, slammed the door, and stomped across the yard to my house without once looking back. This time I didn't care whether my mom had heard the front door slam. She wasn't paying attention anyway.

12

The following Thursday, I received lots of presents for my birthday:

1. An actual birthday card from Robert, not a sympathy card or a Grandparents Day card.

2. A vintage bracelet from the store I'd visited with Delilah. She'd seen me admiring it. I hugged her hard because she was so sweet to notice what I liked—and because she was careful not to give it to me when Addison was around. We hadn't talked about my rocky relationship with Addison, but Delilah must have known things were difficult between us, and she didn't want to make matters worse.

3. A cool beaded necklace from Addison. She seemed genuinely happy when she gave it to me. I could almost ignore the fact that she waited to hand it to me until we were in a crowd, so they could see her being nice to me. Good public relations for her head majorette–elect campaign.

4. A funky patterned baton bag from the majorettes, embroidered with my name. So sweet! And just my style.

5. A text from Carter saying that Max and Addison would not be joining us for our date that night. Carter would meet me at the mall for an early movie, since it was a school night.

It was my *sixteenth birthday*. It was supposed to be my special day. Something so horrible could not be happening! At first I did not want to believe it, and I grasped for alternate explanations. Just because the text *said* it was from Carter didn't mean it *was*. After seeing him three times, I still didn't have his number in my phone.

But when I caught Addison on the football field, she verified the message. Max had texted her to say he couldn't go after all. She fumed because she'd gotten a manicure just for this. It burned me up inside to think that she was worried about her nails, but she never once wondered if something was wrong with Max.

Maybe I *had* read him right last Friday. He really had

gotten up close and personal with Addison because he was jealous of Carter and me. He was so into me that he couldn't stand for us to go out as a group anymore. He couldn't take another night of watching me with Carter.

If so, what should I do about it now?

I would get the chance soon enough to probe Carter about why Max was missing.

In the meantime, right after school, my mom took me to get another birthday gift:

6. My license.

I hadn't been nervous. I'd practically memorized the study guide for the written test. I'd driven enough that I knew I could pass the road test—and after all, who would dare to flunk the chick driving the Aston Martin?

It wasn't until I drove home that it hit me: I could drop off my mom and keep driving by myself!

But I couldn't do that just yet, because I had to get ready for my date with Carter! Bleh.

At home, I opened the first of the four garage doors and very carefully drove the Aston Martin inside. The powerful engine roared even louder in the enclosed space, and I nearly hit the accelerator instead of the brake. In the adjoining garage space, which was usually empty, sat:

7. A brand-new, bright-red Mercedes.

"Is that for me?" I breathed.

My mom nodded, grinning at me. Tears glistened in the corners of her eyes.

"Oh, Mom, thank you!" I threw my arms around her and gave her a big hug.

"Don't thank me," she said. "Your father had it delivered while we were gone."

I tried to maintain my smile as I crossed the space between the cars. Finally I resorted to the majorette grin. The car was gorgeous and I should be grateful. I *was* grateful, but it was hard to be happy when my dad's gift-giving followed such a predictable pattern. He bought expensive cars for women he didn't care about, to keep them off his back.

I opened the heavy door and slid behind the wheel. The interior was white leather. Addison was going to get pink bubblegum on it, and the residue would not come off. I could see it now.

The key was in the ignition. Attached to it was a red ribbon with a handwritten note:

Come see me in Hilton Head.

I was glad my mom had gone inside the house to give me a moment alone with my car. My face probably looked like I was changing into a werewolf as I stared at the note and experienced every emotion I'd ever felt about my dad cheating on my mom and leaving us both.

The idea of driving over to Hilton Head by myself excited me. I was nearly floored by a wave of wanting to hug my dad again and spend a Sunday watching pro football with him. But his girlfriend would be there, and that meant a lot of awkward conversations and strained silences. Kind of like going on a date with Carter.

Well, I owed my dad at least a thank-you for the car. I called him. Holding the phone to my ear, I leaned forward until my head rested on the steering wheel. I listened to the rings and then a recording of his voice, and I left a message.

It was almost time for my date, so I ran inside to grab a sandwich and change. I'd planned to wear my new-to-me bowling shirt, knowing Max would love it. And now he wasn't coming.

I slipped it on anyway and tied a chiffon scarf around my neck for good measure. I knew Carter would hate it, but I was not going to change for him.

I popped my head into my mom's office to say good-bye, ran downstairs, and backed out of the garage in *my car*. I stopped at the mailbox just to check it for cards from my grandmas.

8. Score! Two sweet cards, both with birthday bucks. But there was also:

9. A small, flat package from Max.

Heart going wild, I ripped it open. Inside was a CD. Awww, he had made me a mix CD! I glanced over the song titles, which he'd carefully lettered onto the cover in small, sharp handwriting that seemed so him. Most were birthday rock songs. A few were apology songs. One was a Dolly Paranoids song. I sang through it in my mind, listening for some hidden meaning in the lyrics, like Max was sorry he had chosen the wrong girl to ask out. But I was pretty sure the whole song was about cow tipping.

I opened the case to slip the CD into my player. Inside was a note: *See you tonight!* So, at least when Max had mailed the package, he'd still been planning to come. I wondered again why he had backed out. I hoped he wasn't sick. But I was about to find out.

I drove to the mall and parked in the lot. The evening sun shone too bright. The asphalt had half melted in the late summer heat. I felt queasy, but what was I going to do? I had told Addison I liked Carter. I had told *Max* I liked Carter. It made no sense for me to cancel a date with Carter just because the guy I actually liked was not showing up.

Carter waited for me on a bench outside the multiplex theater. Predictably, his blond brows knitted when he saw me. His head moved up and down, like if he took in my outfit from another angle, he might understand why I was wearing a pink bowling shirt. Beside him on the bench sat:

10. A teddy bear from one of those stores where you made it yourself so you could personalize it to your own tastes, if you were five, or to the tastes of your girlfriend, if you thought she was five. I had been to birthday parties there when I was little. I knew there were lots of animals to choose from, with various clothes and wigs. In fact, there was probably a purple hair option and a majorette costume in there somewhere, but what did I get? A plain brown bear wearing a T-shirt that said I LOVE YOU.

Those three words made me ill. It was the sweetest sentiment, but not one that I shared. As I sat beside Carter on the bench and he kissed me hello, I couldn't imagine he felt that way either. We had never said *I love you* to each other, and yet he was giving it to me on a bear?

I was being petty, which made me mad at myself, which made me more upset. And lest I try to accept the bear graciously and then hide it away forever, it was *huge*, the largest size. Instead of me, Carter, Addison, and Max on my birthday date, it was me, Carter, and taxidermy.

"Aw, Carter," I managed. I did not say, *It's so cute!* because I didn't want to encourage this sort of thing.

He hardly acknowledged my answer. "Good," he said.

Mission accomplished, job over. He stood up and held his hand out to me. "Let's go."

As we walked toward the theater entrance, I asked casually, "So, why couldn't Max come?"

Carter frowned down at me. "Our football team had a scrimmage game at school this afternoon. It didn't go well."

I went cold in the hot evening. "You mean he got hurt?"

Carter shrugged. "I think the only thing hurt was his pride."

I was dying to know what had really happened, but I let it go. I didn't think I could pry the truth out of Carter. I would have to get the story from Max.

Carter and I had the most difficult time carrying on a conversation. Truthfully, a lot of the blame rested with me. I had plenty to tell him. I'd gotten great gifts from my friends, my driver's license, and a frickin' Benz. But I was afraid that if I mentioned my car, he would want to see it, which would drag the date out longer. I never said a word.

He chose the movie. He didn't ask me what I wanted to see, and I didn't realize that he'd chosen without asking me or that he was paying my way until he produced our tickets. It was a slasher film, my very least favorite. He had tried to do something nice for my birthday, but this was not a gift I wanted.

After he handed over the tickets at the door, he went

straight to the concessions line without asking me whether I wanted anything. I didn't. And if I had, I could have bought it myself. Not sure whether he wanted me to stay with him or go away, I waited half a step behind him, edging forward when he advanced in the line. We didn't talk. After he ordered, he turned from the counter holding a vat of soda and a barrel of popcorn. That was par for his usual appetite, so I didn't think much of it.

But after the three of us had settled in our seats—the bear needed one of his own—Carter held the popcorn over the armrest between us, invading my personal space with the warm, buttery aroma, and shook the tub. "Have some."

"No, thanks," I said quickly. I wasn't hungry. At all.

"What do you mean, no thanks? It cost a fortune."

I was stunned. At least the previews were already rolling, so we had an excuse not to argue. I heard Max's voice in my head: I did not like complicated relationships. Maybe I should complicate this one by telling Carter that he shouldn't buy me something I didn't want, then act resentful about it and blame the waste of money on me. But Carter should know this already. And I didn't want to point it out to him, because that might extend our date.

As the movie began, I let my mind wander so I wouldn't have to watch it. I wondered whether Carter had started the argument as an excuse not to kiss me. Because he didn't touch me during the film. Not once.

Finally the credits rolled. Carter placed the popcorn container on the floor. It was empty. He stood and stretched himself to ten or eleven feet. I was about to launch into an excuse for why I needed to leave when he said, "Wow, I'm really beat after our scrimmage today. I hope you don't mind, but I think I'm going to call it a night."

"Oh, that's okay!" I said, trying not to sound ecstatic. We walked outside without another word. Pausing at the edge of the parking lot, we and the bear hugged awkwardly, with no kiss.

I said, "Thanks."

He said, "Happy birthday."

The bear and I walked to the Benz. I looked around to make sure Carter wasn't watching me from across the parking lot, then put the bear in the trunk.

Back in the car, I picked up the envelope Max had sent my CD in and plugged the return address into the GPS on the dashboard. I was surprised at the results. His house and mine were only ten minutes apart. A lot closer than my house and Addison's.

Common sense said I should not go over to my best friend's date's house. But I was not going over there to steal him. This was totally different. In the next few days, when

I found the words, I would call Carter to tell him I didn't want to see him anymore. Addison could find another way to go out with Max—meet him in a well-lighted place that her mom would approve of, or rope another majorette into going out with Carter.

Tonight, I only wanted to see Max to make sure he was okay after his scrimmage.

And to say good-bye.

Max's neighborhood reminded me of the one surrounding Little Five Points, with small yards overflowing with summer flowers. The houses were bungalows from the twenties rather than rambling Victorians. Max's house was gray wood with a rock foundation, a wide front porch, a red door, and white flowers in the window boxes. It looked so sweet that I hated to disturb his happy family with my teen drama.

I might want to say good-bye, but I didn't have to do that at nine o'clock at night. It would look weird to his mom. Depending on whether she was one of those moms who got close to her son's girlfriends, she might mention my visit to Addison. Hell, *Max* might mention it to Addison.

Though I didn't think so.

I pulled into their driveway, behind Max's enormous car, and sat there in the dark for a few minutes, wondering what to do. Should I back out and go home? That was definitely the best plan. But I would not be able to sleep tonight. I would be *tortured* until I settled things with Carter and Max. I couldn't leave yet.

It didn't matter because the decision was made for me. A curtain in Max's house lifted a few inches, letting golden light escape into the dark yard. Someone inside peered at me. Busted! Next the porch lights and the lights lining the sidewalk blinked on, blinding me.

I guessed that meant I was going in. I felt like a juvenile delinquent as I shuffled up the neat sidewalk and rang the bell.

My heart sped up as footsteps approached. The door opened, and Max's mom stood framed in the doorway, holding a microphone.

"Hi," I said. "I'm sorry to come over so late, but I wanted to check on Max and—"

She was looking at my hair. "You're Gemma! Come on this way."

Max had told his mom about me. He must like me! But no—he could have told her Carter's date had striped hair, nothing more. Shutting the front door behind me, I followed Max's mom through the foyer, into the den. Max's dad sat in a recliner with a Japanese newspaper open in front of him. Max's sister wore pajamas and screeched karaoke into her own microphone while she watched her avatar on a video game on TV.

Max was stretched out on the sofa in a T-shirt and track pants, his head cradled on one arm. His other arm, wrapped in a plaster cast, balanced on his stomach. He was sleeping in this room full of racket. I sucked in my breath and moved to stop his mom from waking him.

But she was already stroking his hair and whispering to him in Japanese. He'd told me he couldn't read his T-shirts, but he obviously understood the spoken language. He sat up in a rush and blinked at me. "Cool shirt, Gladys."

I had forgotten I was wearing my new-to-me vintage shirt. For him. "Thanks," I murmured, absolutely certain that no girl had ever blushed this brightly when a boy noticed her bowling shirt. "I'm so sorry. I wouldn't have come over if I'd known you were hurt."

Max's dad had stood and put his newspaper aside. Max stood up too, moving slowly now, like he was sore. His sister had stopped singing and stared at us while the music howled on in the background.

Max glanced uncomfortably around the circle and cleared his throat. "Gemma Van Cleve, this is my dad, Dr. Hirayama, and my mom, the other Dr. Hirayama."

Max's dad smiled, said, "Pleasure," and shook my hand. Max's mom put her hands on her hips. "How come I am the *other* Dr. Hirayama and Daddy gets to be the main one? Why can't Daddy be the *other* Dr. Hirayama?"

Max stared blankly at her. She grinned.

Max gestured to the girl watching us. "And this is my sister, Taylor."

"Are you Max's girlfriend?" Taylor asked. Their mom giggled.

"No," Max and I said at the same time.

"Why not?" Taylor asked.

"You're grounded," Max told her. He turned back to me. "I'm sorry we have to leave. My mother has superhuman hearing, and whatever we say inside the house will get translated into Japanese and repeated on the next seven family-plan phone calls to Tokyo."

"Max!" his mom exclaimed. "I would never embarrass you. That is complete bullshit." His dad started cackling.

Max pressed two fingers between his eyes. "Quick, get me out of here."

"It was so nice to meet everyone!" I sang, pulling him gently by the good arm as I backed toward the door.

They sang back a chorus of good-byes. Max's mom followed us to the door, speaking to Max in Japanese. He nodded. She reached up and pressed her hands on either side of his face, looking into his eyes, then said, "Okay, then. Have fun," and shut the door behind us.

Max jogged down the porch steps like he couldn't get

away from the house fast enough. He stopped short when he saw my car.

"Birthday present from my dad," I said sheepishly. "It's no Aston Martin."

Max laughed heartily at that. "Yeah, but it's . . . wow."

"You want to drive it?" I fished the key fob out of my pocket and held it up.

He shook his head, and his hair fell into his eyes. "I couldn't do that to you. It's your new car, and your birthday."

"I came over to tell you that I'm not going out with Carter anymore," I said. "So this may be your last chance."

Without another word, he took the key from me with his good hand. When he turned the engine over, he grinned. "Grrrrrr," he said along with the motor. We were laughing as he backed out of the driveway and pointed the car down the lamp-lit street.

"So, you're not going out with Carter anymore?" he asked. "I take it your birthday date didn't go well."

"He gave me a bear," I said. "He *made* me a bear wearing an 'I love you' T-shirt."

I expected Max to laugh uproariously at this, like he laughed at just about everything I said, making me feel a hundred percent better about myself. Instead, he frowned at me and said, "That sounds like a good birthday, not a bad birthday."

"I don't love Carter," I said. "And he doesn't love me."

"You make out with him like you do," Max said quietly, watching the road. If I hadn't known better, I would have thought he sounded jealous.

"I don't want to have that argument with you again," I said quickly. "And now that you've pointed it out, I feel ashamed about my reaction to the bear. I should have more appreciation for the bear. Maybe I'm allergic to the stuffing. Or the fur."

"Or sentimentality," Max said.

"Yep." I turned to the window, unable to look at him anymore without crying. Because I was allergic to sentimentality. Yes.

He glanced into the backseat. "Where's the bear? Did you toss him?"

"No! I'm not *that* heartless. He's in the trunk."

Max pulled into a shady park with towering oaks. My cheeks burned at the thought that he wanted to be alone with me here. But as soon as he turned off the engine, he popped the trunk and bailed out of the car, saying, "Let's see this bear."

I met him at the trunk. He opened it, and we stared at the bear lying in the fetal position.

"It's like you're a serial killer," Max said.

"I don't fit the profile."

He gave me a sideways glance. "It's always the quiet ones that fool you. Mild-mannered. Keeps to herself." He closed the trunk and leaned against it, crossing his arms with some difficulty because of the cast. "Have you told Carter you're not going out with him anymore?"

"No, but I will. Maybe you and Addison can arrange some other way to spend time together. You could ingratiate yourself to her mother. Just open the door for her a few times. Mothers love that." I mimicked him, leaning on the trunk and crossing my arms for protection against what I was about to say, and how I was going to expose myself. "I was so sorry you didn't get to come tonight. I realized I looked forward to seeing you more than Carter." Revealing this didn't necessarily tell him I had a crush on him, right?

Regardless, I felt a strong need to change the subject before he could grill me about my feelings for him. I nodded at his cast. "What happened to you?"

"Carter told you I wasn't hurt?"

"He—" I needed to phrase this carefully so I didn't make things worse between them. I didn't want to misrepresent what Carter had said. "He didn't seem sure."

Max nodded sadly, as if this affirmed bad news he already knew. I noticed then how different he looked from last Friday night. This time he hadn't grown a goatee or shaved one off. He looked like he'd aged five years. His eyes were hollow and dark.

"Tell me what happened," I repeated.

Max smiled wanly with one side of his mouth. "You know how there's a penalty in football for roughing the kicker?"

I cringed. The reason there were rules against tackling the kicker, even touching him, was that he was so vulnerable when he kicked, off balance with his foot in the air. He couldn't defend himself against somebody coming at him.

"Fifteen-yard penalty, automatic first down," I said. "Did you get roughed? What did those bastards do to you? I'll kill them for you."

In answer, he held up his cast. "I was trying to protect my leg, so I fell on my hand instead."

I asked dryly, "Was it worth it?"

He looked at me kind of funny. I'd said the wrong thing. Again. Around Max, I never knew how to act. I wanted to be funny so he would like me, at least as a friend. I wanted to act like I didn't care about him, so he wouldn't guess that I watched his eyes for any flicker of affection. Sometimes I tried so hard to be funny that I ended up sounding like an uncaring bitch, the very princess I was afraid of being. Which might have been true of me about some things, but not about this. Not about Max.

If he was thinking how cold I was, he laughed it off the next moment. "No, it wasn't worth it at *all*. I made the field goal, so we took the points and declined the penalty anyway."

"That's sweet revenge. At least you made the goal. Is your arm broken?" To make up for acting like I didn't care, I went a little overboard. I reached out for his cast. He moved it nearer. I supported it with my palm.

"My wrist," he said.

"Can you play?"

"Yeah, I can play. My mom doesn't want me to, but I'm going to. Coach says the next guy on the team who hits me or allows a hit on me is off the team, so I think I'm safe now."

Nobody should have allowed a hit on him, especially during a scrimmage when they were playing *themselves*. But to say the next person who allowed a hit on Max was off the team . . . that was saying a lot. The coach saw something in Max and wanted to keep him.

"Does it hurt?" I asked.

"Yep." I could tell by his curt answer that it hurt a *lot*.

"Does your hand still work?"

Ever so slowly he turned his wrist over in my palm. The cast whispered against my skin as he slid his hand down. We were holding hands.

No, he was just giving me a demonstration of the fabulous, still intact workings of his digits. And even if we were holding hands, I was in the eleventh grade, and there was absolutely no reason for my face and arms to tingle or my mind and heart to race. I couldn't slow my breathing, but I tried to pant quietly so he wouldn't notice.

"Anyway, it's over now," he said, as if it wasn't a big deal that we were holding hands. And maybe it wasn't. But I was dating his best friend—or at least, I had been—and he was still dating mine.

"I'm sorry I missed your birthday date," he went on. "I was at the hospital getting X-rays. Maybe I should show them to Carter. I guess he thought I was faking."

"There's more to it than that," I prompted him.

Max grimaced.

"Tell me," I said.

He sighed the longest sigh. "I can't prove it, of course, but I'm pretty sure it happened because Carter's always telling the team what a wuss I am. He didn't actually order that guy to hit me, but he might as well have."

I nodded. Judging from the way Carter constantly attacked Max in front of Addison and me, Max was probably right.

"Carter's not the team captain," Max said. "A senior is, but as quarterback, Carter has a lot of sway. I already knew the damage was done and the team didn't respect me, but I didn't realize how bad the damage was until they came after me on the field. I don't know of any way to undo it."

I asked quietly, "Are you afraid you'll get hurt again and you won't be able to play?"

"I'm afraid I've lost my mojo," he admitted. "I'm afraid I'll never make another kick. Part of me thinks that if I can't, it serves me right. The great kickers are the ones who don't get rattled. That's football."

"Kickers aren't usually hit," I pointed out, "especially by their own teammates in a scrimmage. You shouldn't second-guess yourself because of it."

"Yeah." He nodded. I could tell he agreed with me, in theory. He knew his team was at fault, not him, but he didn't *feel* it, and his mojo had everything to do with *feeling* it.

He looked up at me for the first time in a while, eyes sad. "This is crazy, but I really wanted to kick for Georgia Tech."

"That's not crazy."

He shrugged. "They're not the greatest team in the world, but they have their years."

"They won the national championship in 1990, sort of."

"Right! They had to share it with Colorado."

"Some years," I said, "the kicker might be the only

player putting any points on the scoreboard. On the bright side, you'd get a lot of respect from the quarterback."

Max laughed bitterly, let go of my hand, and tried to run both hands back through his hair to push it out of his eyes. He'd forgotten that one arm was in a cast. He put both hands down.

"When this happened," I asked carefully, "did you get mad?"

"Ha," he said. "Yeah."

"As mad as you got at Addison last week?"

He colored in the faint glow of the streetlight. "There were a lot of things going on that night, and then what Addison said caught me off guard. I would never lose it like that in front of the team."

"Good," I said. "Sometimes the way a guy reacts can just feed the fire, you know? He gets so upset that other guys just want to come after him more." That's what Robert and his friends did to freshman boys in the band. The more upset the boys got, the more fun they were to torture.

"I know better," Max said. "I have experience with being bullied."

"So after you got hit, you looked like you do now," I guessed. "Half smiling with your jaw locked, like you're very angry and holding your breath and waiting for it all to be over."

"Probably." His jaw locked again.

"That's how you looked in the car when you drove me home last Friday, right after you kissed Addison."

I flushed hot with embarrassment the instant the words left my mouth. I had hoped he'd kissed her only to make me jealous, because he was angry after watching me kiss Carter. But I was way out on a limb, voicing this suspicion.

Max's brows were down, and his dark eyes held mine.

My heart sped up. It knew what was about to happen, even if I didn't.

Max reached his good hand behind my head. His fingers slid across the nape of my neck and interlaced themselves in my hair.

He set his forehead against mine, resting there for a moment, making sure I wouldn't pull away and I wanted this as much as he did.

I cradled his jaw in my hand.

And then he kissed me.

13

This kiss was not tentative like my first kiss with Carter. It was deep immediately. I kissed Max back with the same passion. I had never felt so good in my life.

We leaned against the trunk, with his casted arm sandwiched awkwardly between us. He moved it behind my back. Now we were not only face-to-face but chest-to-chest, thigh-to-thigh. I put both arms around his neck and pulled him even closer. He groaned and slid his good hand out of my hair and down my back.

We kissed that way for a long time. It still felt awkward, standing against the back of the car. But I was afraid that if we stopped, Max would remember Addison, and that would be the end of this. I was going to feel terribly guilty about making out with my best friend's boyfriend, later. But not right now. Not when my blood sparkled in my veins like this.

It was Max who finally broke the kiss and rested his forehead against mine again, panting a little against my lips. "Let's make better use of this car."

Heat flashed through me. Obediently I let him go and backed around the car, putting my hand on the passenger door.

He looked across the roof at me from the driver's side, but he didn't have his hand on the front door like I did. He had his hand on the back door. He growled, "That is not what I meant, Gemma."

My hand was trembling as I reached for the other door handle. We closed ourselves into the backseat and met in the middle of all that white leather.

We kissed for a long time, slowly learning each other. Max spent some quality time experimenting with my ear, chuckling every time he found a new way to make me shudder. Chill bumps broke out all over my skin.

Then he slid his hand down to my waistband. Still kissing me, he gently tugged the tail of my shirt out of my shorts. One-handed, he fumbled with opening the lowest button of my shirt, then the next, then the next. Though it was warm in the car, the air felt strangely cold breezing against my stomach. He warmed my bare skin with his hand.

I was not the least bit self-conscious about him touching my waist. I liked being close to Max. But as his hands traveled upward, toward my bra, I kissed him less and shuddered more. Addison had let a guy touch her there *last year*. I should be ready to let Max feel me up, but I wasn't. He was the second boy I'd kissed in my whole life.

"No?" Max's hand stopped on my skin. He pulled away and whispered, "We don't have to." But his expression was serious, and he did not take his hand off me. He would stop if I told him to stop, but he didn't want to stop.

I didn't want to either. I just wanted more time. Next time, maybe, or the time after that. And I wished that I could tell him this. But as I looked into his eyes, I remembered this would probably be the last time I saw Max.

Our relationship was very, very complicated.

"Let me instead," I suggested.

He nodded and smoothed his hand down my belly, out from under my shirt. His hand was shaking.

I placed my hands between his T-shirt and his hot skin. He jumped at my touch. As he watched me with his black hair hanging in his dark eyes, he had never looked more sexy, and I had never been more in love with him.

Slowly I worked his T-shirt over his head and off him.

I straddled his lap with his strong, bare arms encircling me and kissed him again. I trailed my kisses down his neck and dragged my lips across his chest. My adrenaline spiked every time he gasped. I began to have second thoughts about not letting him put his hands where he wanted.

But time was up. Glancing at my watch, I said sadly, "I have to go. My curfew is early on school nights."

"Damn it." Max tightened his hard arms around me and rubbed his cheek against mine. "I don't want you to go."

I didn't want to talk about leaving, because it would lead to a talk about not seeing each other anymore. My head filled with what we would say. Maybe one of us would suggest meeting again behind Addison's back. Which reminded me of what my dad must have said once upon a time to his girlfriend, when he was still married to my mom.

Instead, I said lightly, "Why'd you shave your goatee?"

"It was itchy when I put my helmet on."

I ran my thumb along his stubbly chin, where the goatee had been. "Why'd you grow it in the first place?"

"I thought you might like it."

I giggled. "You thought right. I did like it. I like you without it too. Why don't you grow it back sometime? We can test which way I like better."

I stopped stroking his chin. That was exactly what I was trying *not* to do, hint at what came next for us. Or not.

"That sounds like a plan." He kissed my cheek, then my lips, seemingly oblivious to the problem that stood in front of us like a roadblock.

I sat up straighter on his lap, one hand centered on his bare chest, and looked him in the eye. "Wait a minute. What do you mean, you grew a goatee because you thought I might like it? That was before you went out with Addison."

He blinked. "I've wanted you all along, not her. But could we make out some more before we have that conversation? You're going to be kind of mad." He closed his eyes and kissed my lips again.

I scooted off his lap. "Max. If you liked me this whole time, why'd you go out with Addison?" I meant to keep my voice even, but the end of my question came out as a whine, filled with all the frustration I'd felt during the last three weeks.

He crossed his muscular arm and his casted arm over his lean chest. "If you bought your Studio 54 shirt because you knew I would like it, why did you go out with Carter?"

I opened my mouth, then closed it again. I had plenty to say, but I was too outraged to say it. Finally I managed, "I was with Carter because *you asked Addison out*!"

"I did not!" he exclaimed.

"Addison told me you did."

"No! You must have misunderstood her. No."

I had not misunderstood Addison. I knew this in my heart.

But Max went on earnestly, "I saw you from across the football field at camp. I thought you noticed me, too. When camp was over, I asked Carter to wait with me so I could try to talk to you on your way out."

"And Addison talked to you instead," I griped.

"Well, you got hit in the nose," he said, gently touching where Addison had clobbered me. "I thought that quieted you down. I was going to try to talk to you at the Varsity, but you got sullen, remember? And then, when you left the table to text your mom, I suggested to Addison that the four of us could go out together. I was afraid if I asked you out by yourself, you'd say no, because we'd just met and you'd mentioned serial killers. I figured if we went out as a group first, I might grow on you, and then I could make my move on you."

"That's not what Addison told me," I said, so frustrated now that I could have cried. "She specifically told me that *you* had asked *her* out, and that I had to go out with Carter so her mother would let her out of the house."

Max shook his head. "I have no idea where she got that."

I knew where she had gotten it. Addison had seen something she'd wanted, and she'd lied to get it.

Max pointed at me. "But then she came back to the table and said that *you* thought Carter was fine!"

I stared at Max for a few moments with my mouth open, not quite believing what I was hearing. "I said Carter was *fine*?"

"That's what Addison said." Max glared at me accusingly.

"I did not say that," I insisted. "When she told me you'd asked her out, she said she wanted me to go out with Carter. She asked me if I liked him. I may have said that I *liked him fine*."

He sighed suddenly like he'd been holding his breath. "So she just misheard you. She wasn't lying."

"She was totally lying, trust me."

His brows went down like he disapproved of my comment.

I was so angry that I hardly noticed, and I definitely didn't care. "How could you believe I said Carter was *fine*?" I protested. "That doesn't sound like anything I'd say about anybody. That is a strange expression *Addison* would use."

"I didn't know that. I'd just met you."

"But Max! Why would you still want to go out with me if you believed I said it?"

"I had my misgivings. But you were too perfect, and I couldn't let you go just because you thought you liked Carter. I knew he wasn't into you. He knew I was. And I could tell he had a thing for Addison but didn't want to admit it. He was too wrapped up in moping about his ex-girlfriend. So I kicked him under the table a few times to make him go along with the plan."

Max reached out to finger the embroidered GLADYS on my shirt pocket. "Then, in the MARTA station, you said the tile art of the countryside was ironic, and I was hooked again. I had to have you. When we got home, I called Carter and convinced him that if we all went out together, we could switch it up and make it right."

I took in Max's handsome, shadowed face, the gold pendant on a red cord around his neck, the chiseled muscles of his arms and chest. After all the weeks I'd pined for him, this revelation was too good to be true, and I did not quite believe it. "You never liked Addison?" I repeated.

"No."

I thought back to our first date, meeting her and Carter in the shopping center parking lot. "You were staring at her cleavage, Max."

"How could I help it? *Everybody* was staring at her cleavage. *You* were staring at her cleavage."

I laughed bitterly at that, because it was true. "And this is why you kept throwing darts at me, like at Little Five Points when you made fun of the way I dress. You were mad at me for liking Carter."

He opened his hands. "Because why would you like Carter instead of me? You were supposed to be with *me*!"

I felt ill. "This is what you and Carter have been arguing about."

"Like we didn't have enough already," Max grumbled. "Yes. He was supposed to go out with you, if that's what you wanted, but not to stick his tongue down your throat. He's been doing that because he knew it infuriated me and I couldn't do anything." Max's eyes blazed fire.

"Why did Carter go out with me tonight, then, when you couldn't?"

"I told him he had to. It was your birthday. I didn't want you to get stood up."

"Thanks, Max," I said sarcastically, thinking of the heartfelt gift of the slasher film. "Was that 'I love you' bear your idea?"

"I told him to give you *something* for your birthday. His ex-girlfriend gave that back to him, I think."

Max still sat in front of me, but all I could see was Addison, lips pursed and fists balled in excitement as she told me her great news in the Varsity, every bit of which was a lie to steal *my guy*.

"I hate Addison," I said. "I hate her with every fiber of my being. I have never hated anyone like I hate that girl, not even my dad's girlfriend. I would seriously like to put hair remover in her shampoo."

I took a long, ragged breath. The anger relented a little. Max stared at me with his nostrils flared like I was some distasteful lower species—the way the cool, popular kids used to look at me when I was younger and I passed by their table in the lunchroom.

"Good to know." He found his shirt balled on the floorboard, turned it right side out, and jerked it on. "I'm sorry to have put you through all this trouble, Gemma. I can tell now that it's not going to work out." He got out of the car.

"What?" Alarmed, I shoved open my door and met him at the hood. "What do you mean it's not going to work out?"

He kept walking around to the passenger side. "I make girls mad. I make you mad too, but you kept coming back for more. You understood me. That's what I thought, anyway." He opened the passenger door. "I fell in love with you, Gemma. I've been waiting to tell you that every waking moment for the last three weeks. I love you. And all you can focus on is that you're angry at Addison!" He slammed the door behind him.

I stood there in a huff, trying to calm down, staring at his scowl through the windshield. With a sharp breath I looked up at the tops of the oak trees towering overhead and disappearing into the starlight. He was right. I was so angry at Addison that there was hardly room in my brain for anything else. She had fooled me and used me and tricked me out of being with the guy I wanted most in the world. But if I didn't snap out of it, I was going to lose him permanently.

A cool breeze swept through the trees. I shivered, then realized I was standing in a public park with my shirt unbuttoned and my bra showing. I buttoned up, glancing once at Max. He was watching me.

I walked to the driver's side and slid behind the wheel. Starting the engine with a roar, I said, "We have got to solve this, Max, but it's a school night and I have to go."

He waved his casted arm in the air, dismissing the problem. "There's nothing to solve."

"Don't say that," I insisted, turning onto the road to his house.

So he didn't. But he didn't say anything else, either. We sat in stubborn silence all the way back to his house. My lips still tingled from kissing him. My skin tingled where his hot hand had touched me. I could not *believe* Addison had made me wait three weeks for Max, and tortured me by making me think I would *never* have him.

And now I never would.

As I parked in Max's driveway, I didn't want my anger to get the better of me. The more times that happened, the angrier I got at Addison, which just fed the fire. I took a deep breath and tried one more time.

"Max. Just because you think you have it all figured out doesn't mean it's true. You're not always right."

"Really?"

"Really. What we did for the past hour . . . that was real between us. That was not some scheme to get revenge on Addison, at least not on my end. Didn't it feel real to you? I could not fake that with you."

He nodded. "So you've liked me all this time, from when we first met at camp. You weren't trying to get back at Addison. You liked me for me."

"Yes!"

"Just like it was real and you didn't fake it when you made out with Carter last Friday, and the Friday before that."

I took a breath to tell him the truth. When I'd been with Carter, I'd been trying to make the best out of a bad situation.

"You're not going to be with me," Max said, his voice a sexy, menacing rumble over the roar of the engine. "You won't win your game with Addison this time. By next year, all the two of you will remember is that you had an argument about some guy, but you won't remember me or exactly why. I'm not even a real person to you. To you, it's all about getting one up on Addison."

"That is not true, Max," I whispered with tears in my eyes, because it wasn't. I reached across the car for him.

He opened the door and backed out, pulling away from my hand. "You thought you were hungry, but then you decided, no, you really just wanted something to eat." He slammed the door behind him.

14

Friday was such a big day for me. That night I would perform for the first time ever as a majorette! I'd ironed my clothes for school several days beforehand, and caught up on my homework so I could sleep as long as possible the morning of my big day. And wouldn't you know, I hardly slept at all. I woke up hours early, all with one thing in mind: telling Addison off.

By that time I'd obsessed all night and planned the attack carefully. I did not want to wait until band. That would mean I had to live with the anger cycling over and over in my mind for almost the whole school day. I didn't have any other classes with her, so I had to catch her before the first bell rang, when everybody walked from their cars or the buses and gathered on the grass in front of the school.

I found a parking space—not as easy as it sounded, since it was my first time driving myself to school—and jogged around the building to the front lawn. Addison was laughing with the other majorettes, chatting them up before the vote. That made me even angrier. On top of everything else she'd done to me, when she won head majorette–elect that night, she would officially be the boss of me!

I felt like I was on some trashy, staged reality show as I headed for her, like everybody on the lawn was watching me and laughing at me. But probably nobody was actually looking at me until I stomped up to the majorettes and told Addison, "I need to talk to you alone."

She looked at me and blinked her eyes innocently. "Why?"

I had been friends with Addison for a long time. I usually knew when she was lying to me. I hadn't known when she told me that Max had asked her out—maybe because I wasn't in a mental place where I could believe he liked me then—but I knew now that she was guilty. Something in her eyes gave her away. Either Max had told her about last night, or she had figured out that we were together.

"You know why," I said quietly.

She gestured to the other majorettes, who looked at us

curiously. "There's nothing you need to say to me that you can't say to my friends."

So now they were her friends, not mine.

I glanced at the five of them, watching me expectantly. My gaze rested on Delilah, whose black eyes were huge and full of horror. If Addison wanted me to say this in front of them, so be it.

"You lied to me." Those words felt so good to say that it was easy for me to keep going. "You told me Max asked you out when he didn't. You knew I liked him first." I heard my own voice rising. I sensed people from across the school yard crowding behind me to watch this spectacle, which was exactly what I hadn't wanted. Some wise-ass yelled, "Fight!"

I knew I was in trouble when Addison looked triumphant. "Your boyfriend is *Carter*!" she crowed. "If you like Max now, you stole *my* boyfriend! You have been double dipping!"

The crowd gasped.

"I have not been doing any such thing!" I hollered at her. "That is dirty. It doesn't mean what you think it means."

She put her hands on her hips, uncomfortable for the first time. "Oh yeah? And how do you know all these expressions if you haven't been *doing* something dirty?"

"Because I am in band, and I am friends with trumpets!" I must have sounded as crazy as I felt, screaming this at her, because someone stepped behind me and put a steadying hand on my back.

"You are in big trouble, Gemma Van Cleve," Addison sneered at me. She touched her nose with her fingertip. At first I thought she was reminding me that she'd broken my nose so long ago. Or she was rubbing in how ugly my nose was now.

Instead, she said, "You didn't keep your nose clean."

She turned and flounced across the yard and into school. Toward the band room. Toward Mrs. Baxter.

"Ooooooh," said the crowd.

The person attached to the calming hand on my back stepped forward. It was Robert. "Show's over, folks. Nothing to see here." He waved his hands like he was shooing cows. Several of them actually mooed as they dispersed.

He bent to look into my eyes. "Are you okay? What was that all about?"

"Yeah!" The head majorette leaned close, bringing the rest of the majorettes with her. "You always keep calm and carry on, Gemma. If *you're* involved in drama, it must be serious."

I was going to brush it off and tell them, "Nothing," but that would be a lie. And as I looked around and saw their concern, I realized they really were my friends. I wanted them to know what had happened.

So I told them the bare bones of the story. The truth, so that Addison couldn't accuse me of spreading rumors about her.

"And *she's* going to try to get you kicked off the majorette squad for *that*?" Delilah squeaked. "She can't do that!"

"I guess she can," I said, defeated. "We all knew what Mrs. Baxter's rules were when we tried out."

The bell rang, and we hiked up the stairs to the school. As I sat in a series of quiet classrooms, alone with my thoughts except for the occasional Pythagorean theorem or genealogy of the British royal family, I calmed down. I felt better about what had happened. I *was* relieved that I had confronted Addison. I had accused her of this one transgression, but that was all it took to purge my bitterness about a six-year friendship full of insults and slights. I was gratified that Robert had taken up for me and the majorettes had not abandoned me. I hoped that only a few people had witnessed the fight.

That hope was dashed as I walked from class to class. I was almost late for dance because so many people stopped me to ask if I'd really dated the quarterback *and* the kicker from the rival team. Technically I had never gone on a date with Max, so I said no. Which felt like a betrayal of him, even though our night together had ended awfully.

I dreaded going to band. Addison would be there, and she would confront me again. Mrs. Baxter would be there, and she would tell me I was off the squad. Expecting something horrible to happen was almost worse than it actually happening. I spent the whole sweltering hour in that excruciating limbo. I was so distracted that I dropped my baton. Twice.

Mrs. Baxter never called me out of the line. But she seemed to scowl at me more disapprovingly than usual. I couldn't be sure because she and the band director viewed us from so high in the stands. But Addison was only five yards away from me, with the other majorettes gathered around her. She was *definitely* scowling.

The next time the band ran the drill, we all moved to new positions on the field, and I was a long way from Addison. I looked around for Delilah to ask her what was going on. She was already walking toward me.

"You told us you liked the kicker for East in the first place, instead of the quarterback," she said. "But you're not with the kicker *now*. Are you?"

I tried to read her expression. When we'd gone to the vintage store, she'd guessed that I'd fallen for a guy I was going out with that night. I just hadn't clued her in that the guy was Max instead of Carter. I hoped she understood that I couldn't have told her then, because Max had belonged to Addison. Or so I'd thought.

"I'm not dating either of them now," I said. Seven words, and so much behind them.

"Good," she said. "If you were dating the kicker, I would have been worried. Since you're not, this is probably good news."

I doubted it.

"This morning Addison was talking about turning you in to Mrs. Baxter," Delilah said. "Now she's talking about getting revenge on the kicker instead. Maybe you're off the hook."

"How is she getting revenge on him?" I hated to ask.

"She says he's really superstitious about game days."

"Yeah," I whispered.

"She's sending flowers to his house this afternoon," Delilah said. "She acts like that's going to get him good, but I don't see how it will ruin his game, do you? Are flowers bad luck?"

"Only in context," I murmured. "He's superstitious about kicking, and his game day has to go like every other game day. I'd be willing to bet nobody ever sent him flowers before."

Delilah touched my arm. "You really care about him."

I nodded as tears filled my eyes. I was not going to cry. Not while Addison was glaring across the field at me and talking behind her hand to another majorette.

"Then you should discuss it with Addison," Delilah said. "I'm sure she'll listen to reason. Come on, I'll go with you." She tugged at my shirt.

I shook my head. If Delilah thought Addison would listen to reason, she didn't know Addison very well. "I have another way to take care of it."

My first idea was to camp out at Max's house and wait for the florist truck so I could intercept it. But I didn't know when Max would be home. I couldn't be there when he arrived. I was the girl he'd gotten together with and made out with and dumped the night before. Finding me in his driveway would probably be even more unusual and traumatic for him on game day than receiving a bouquet of flowers. I didn't have Dr. Hirayama's number or the other Dr. Hirayama's number, but I had Carter's.

Thinking hard about this, I missed my baton twice more during practice, and I caught Mrs. Baxter shaking her head at me from the stands. Finally, after practice was over, I waited until everyone had filed out of the stadium with their instruments and I had the whole field to myself. I called Carter, hoping he would actually answer. He might not have turned his ringer back on after school.

He might see my name and ignore the call, thinking I was asking him out on a date. He might—

"Hey, Gemma," he said quickly.

After a little pause of surprise, I said, "Hey!"

"I know you're calling because Addison told you," he said. "We shouldn't have done it when I hadn't talked to you first. But Max told me this morning that y'all were making out at the same time Addison and I were, so I don't see the problem. I mean, I know you and Max aren't together now, but . . ."

I gathered from this non-apology that he had gone over to Addison's house and sucked face with her last night, right after my birthday movie complete with I LOVE YOU bear. And no, Addison *hadn't* told me. She had let me think *I* was the evil one. She had told *Mrs. Baxter* I was the mean one. I hated her so much at that moment that I could hardly see the goalpost at the far end of the football field.

But I was on a mission, and I fought through that anger to remember why I'd called Carter. I cleared my throat. "I'm surprised you and Max are speaking to each other after the scrimmage yesterday. His version of the story was different from yours."

Now Carter paused for a moment before saying slowly, "He's not exactly speaking to me. He yelled at me across chemistry class and got sent out in the hall. He's pretty upset about how things ended with you."

"But you still care about his mojo, right?" I asked. "You act like you don't care about *him*, but you care how he kicks for your team."

I took his silence for a reluctant yes.

"Addison is trying to mess with his mojo," I said. "She's sending flowers to his house. I need you to intercept them. It would be pretty normal for you to hang out at his house before a game, right? Or warn his parents about the flowers. Whatever it takes to keep Max from seeing them."

Carter was quiet so long that I thought he was going to say no. I took a breath to tell him what being best friends with someone meant. Like I knew.

He spoke before I could. "Why would Addison do that?" he asked. "Does she still like him?"

I didn't think Addison had the hots for Max. Not since he'd started making good jokes. I said carefully, "Addison is dramatic."

"Yeah, she is." Carter laughed. "I love that about her."

I was glad *someone* did. "So, will you intercept the flowers? I know you think Max is silly to be superstitious. But you're not going to change that about him by tonight's game."

"Yeah, I'll do it," he said. "Thanks for letting me know. And Gemma? I'm sorry about the popcorn."

This made so little sense to me that I almost said, *And I am sorry about the pumpernickel, and the backhoe.*

"At the movie last night," he reminded me. "I knew you wouldn't want popcorn because you're careful about what you eat. I bought it to make you mad. I was so into Addison, and I felt like you had messed everything up by liking me. I was trying to make you stop."

He had done a great job. "That's okay, Carter. I'm just glad that you and Addison are together now." I said this with no irony in my voice.

"I hope you and Max can work things out," Carter said. "I'll tell him you called to warn me about this."

"No!" I insisted. "That's definitely never happened on his game day before. I don't want to mess with his mojo."

"Then he won't know you did something nice for him," Carter argued.

I winced. Carter was right. Max really hated me right now, and letting him know that I'd tried to protect him might help heal that wound.

But it wasn't worth it. I told Carter, "His mojo is more important."

After we hung up, I pocketed my phone and picked up my batons. I performed an illusion, a one-turn, a two-turn, and a figure eight, every trick that had caused me to drop a baton during practice. I performed them over and over until I was absolutely certain I had regained my confidence.

Finally I jogged up the steps, out of the empty stadium, into the empty parking lot. I walked to my pretty car, gleaming red in the bright sunshine. "Grrrrr," I growled as I started the engine, remembering the delight in Max's eyes when he had driven it.

I knew he was angry at me. I understood why. But we'd had too much fun together in the past few weeks, and we'd made each other feel too good last night, for either of us to walk away now. We'd never even been on a date! At least, not with each other.

Max had told me he loved me. I hadn't gotten the chance to tell him back.

As I thought about making up with him, shivers raced down my arms. I turned off the air-conditioning and opened the windows to the hot wind and the smells of late summer flowers and traffic. Maybe Carter would tell Max about what I'd done to save his mojo—*after* the game. That would help Max forgive me. And Carter had said Max had yelled at him in chemistry. At least I knew Max still felt strongly about me. That was step one.

I'd talked myself into an optimistic mood by the time I parked my car in the garage. Skipping into the kitchen, I was about to dump my book bag and take my batons outside to practice a little more when I heard my mother's footsteps coming down the stairs. Something must be wrong. She never emerged from her office just because I came home.

She was wearing her business suit, heels, expensive perfume, and a frown. "Tell me your side of the story quickly, Gemma, and I'll do what I can for you." She grabbed her purse from a hook by the door.

"What do you mean?" I breathed.

She put her hands on her hips. "Mrs. Baxter didn't tell you? She wants to kick you off the majorette line. Something about keeping your nose clean?"

I swallowed. "That bitch."

"Gemma!" my mom exclaimed.

"Not Mrs. Baxter," I grumbled.

My mom glanced at her watch. "Sit down at the table. I'll heat up some cobbler right quick, and we'll talk about it."

I stamped my foot like a ten-year-old girl. "I don't want cobbler!" I screamed at her. "I want you!"

And I burst into tears.

15

To my mom's credit, she didn't lose it. One of us had to hold it together. She guided me into the library, pushing me gently from behind as I stumbled along, blinded by tears. We sank onto the leather sofa, and I cried into her lap.

After a few minutes, when I was mostly cried out, I told her the whole story of Max and Carter and Addison and me. It sounded stupid to my own ears, like a list of Poor Teen Decisions from tenth-grade health class. What had set this chain of events in motion was the sight of Max at camp, long black hair in his eyes, body hard and lean, kicking goal after goal through the uprights. And Max wasn't here, so I couldn't expect any of this to ring true to my mom.

But she had met Max, and maybe that was why the story seemed to make some sense to her. When I finished with a gargantuan sniffle, she said, "This is my fault. We don't have to eat cobbler together, or even eat dinner together every night, but we should be talking every day. I should know who you're going out with." She put her hands up, stopping herself. "I *did* know who you were going out with. I should know which one you *like*."

She used one finger to pull a purple strand of hair out of my eyes. "We will start over. We will be closer, starting now. Okay?"

I nodded. I wished I could have told her how relieved I felt when she said this, but I was all talked out.

She sat back and grimaced at me. "I never have approved of the way Addison treats you. I'm surprised you're still friends with that girl."

I wiped my wet eyes. "What are you talking about? You *made* me be friends with her."

"I certainly did not!" my mom exclaimed.

"You made me take baton lessons with her when we were ten!" I cried.

Her brow furrowed, thinking. "Did I?"

"Yes! You told me poor Addison didn't want to take baton by herself."

She sighed and leaned back against the sofa. "Your father had just left, Gemma, and you were moping around the house. He wasn't taking you to football games anymore, or on hikes and bike rides, and you had stopped playing outside with the other kids in the neighborhood. I'd loved baton when I was young. I thought it would be something fun for you to do to get some exercise, and Addison was doing it too, and her parents were divorcing. You'd have a friend who was going through some of the same things you were going through. I don't remember how I put it to you, but maybe I did say 'poor Addison,' just to convince you to try it. You seemed so unhappy, and I was frustrated that I couldn't do anything to make it better."

She looked down at her lap. I thought she would start crying. I sniffled again and prepared to dry up so I could comfort her instead of the other way around.

But she was only checking her watch again. She reached out and framed my face with her hands—just as Max's mom had held him the night before. "You relax for a while, eat a good supper, and put on your majorette outfit, pretty girl. I will speak to Mrs. Baxter and take care of this for you."

"I don't see how," I wailed. "Majorettes have to keep their noses clean, and I knew that going into this. It's a rule."

"It's a sexist rule," she snapped. "You don't see anybody

at Max's high school trying to kick *him* off the football team for kissing *you*, do you? That would be ridiculous, right?"

"Right," I said with more enthusiasm than I felt.

"Mrs. Baxter will not kick you off the squad for this, Gemma, I promise." She patted my knee. "You've worked too hard, and I will stand up for you. If I have to, I'll threaten a lawsuit."

"That won't help," I moped. "A lawsuit would take months. Years."

"The lawsuit might, but the threat is instant." My mom grinned. "I'll drive to the front of the school and park in the principal's space in my Aston Martin."

We both giggled as she stood and crossed the library. But when she turned in the doorway, her face was serious again. "And in case that doesn't work, I will have a long talk with Addison's mother."

The game was held at Max's school this year, so we were the away band. That meant the majorettes' only performance before halftime was marching into the stadium to the drum cadence—which still involved a lot of kicks and horizontal spins. It was easy to drop your baton if you weren't paying attention. Nobody had a drop but Addison. She dropped hers twice. When we got to the stands, she cried and made a big dramatic deal out of it like her life was ruined.

I couldn't worry about her. I was too busy watching the game. I wanted my team to win, but I also wanted *Max* to win. There had been no nail-biters yet. He hadn't been called on to make a kick for points—no field goal for him, but no extra point for one of Carter's touchdowns, either. Max had only performed a few flawless kickoffs and punts. Even among the identical football uniforms and helmets, he was easy to pick out with his casted arm. If it hadn't been for that, I still would have recognized him by the way he walked.

And in between plays, I was trying to talk Delilah out of fainting.

"You were fine during tryouts," I reminded her. "That decided whether you would be a majorette or not, so that was a lot more stressful than a game."

"That was in front of twelve hundred people," she wailed. "This is in front of five thousand. Plus, at tryouts, I watched you in the stands the whole time. You kept me calm."

"Watch your parents," I suggested.

"They are judging me," she whispered.

I looked over my shoulder, craning my neck toward the stands behind the fifty yard line. "Watch my mom." I pointed her out. I drew my hand back in surprise at the sequins covering my arm and catching the light, then laughed at myself and pointed again. "My mom is there next to the aisle, six rows down, in pink. She will not judge you. She will support you. Doesn't she look sweet?"

Looks could be deceiving, though. My mom might act sweet to most people, but she'd made her point at the school. Mrs. Baxter had given me a bigger hug for luck than any other majorette before we marched into the stadium. She was very careful not to look askance at my purple-striped curls artfully arranged around my tiara.

And my mom had made her point to Addison's mom too. Right before the game, Addison had called me to apologize.

There was a commotion around us as the head majorette, Susan, stood and made her way down the row to the aisle. The band officers from Max's high school had walked over to our side of the stadium for the traditional second-quarter visit. I peered at their drum major in his green and gold military uniform. We wore red and blue, but otherwise, the bands looked a lot alike. I wondered whether Max was friends with their majorette squad, and whether he had made any of these girls mad.

"Gemma!"

Susan was motioning to me. Squeezing Delilah's knee to comfort her, I slid past her and clopped down the aisle in my knee-high boots to the band officers. The East band's head majorette and another majorette were grinning at me.

"It's Gemma, all right," the head majorette said, looking at my hair. "It's so great to finally meet you in person! I'm LaShondra, and this is Val."

"Boy, have we heard a lot about *you*!" Val exclaimed.

"From Max," LaShondra added.

"Really?" I asked, trying not to seem too eager. "Carter told me he and Max had an altercation in chemistry."

"They did," Val said knowingly, like it had been something to see.

"Carter told me Max got sent out in the hall," I said.

LaShondra waved one glittering arm dismissively. "Yeah, but Max talks in class a lot. He pretty much lives out in the hall."

"We've been hearing about you for longer than that," Val said.

LaShondra said, "First day of school, he corners me and says, 'LaShondra! I met this *girl*! She goes to West, she has purple streaks in her hair, she's really funny, she twirls batons like they are part of her, and I have never seen a girl so hot.'"

Val cackled. "You sound just like him!"

It *was* a good imitation of Max—so good it almost made me tear up, thinking about him. "He may have felt that way before, but we had a pretty big argument last night."

Val shook her head. "He still feels that way. He picked me up to bring me to the game, and he told me to tell you hi."

I put a hand over the warmth in my chest. "Awww! That is so sweet!"

"You're going to get back with him, right?" LaShondra asked.

I nodded. "I hope. I didn't want to talk to him on game day and mess with his mojo."

I thought I might have to explain what I meant by Max's mojo. But they both said, "Ohhhh," nodding, and stepped back a pace.

"He's very superstitious about kicking," LaShondra said.

Our drum major blew a couple of blasts on his whistle, which meant that the band had to file out of the stands and line up in the end zone for the halftime show. The majorettes from East waved to me as they walked away, and LaShondra mouthed, *Good luck*. I made my way back to my seat to retrieve my batons. The butterflies that had been living in my stomach all day were growing into a small species of bird.

In contrast, Delilah seemed okay. It wasn't until we were in place in the end zone and the scoreboard showed one minute to halftime that she started hyperventilating. We were supposed to be standing at attention, which for majorettes meant both batons on our hips and our grins cemented to our faces. But I couldn't ignore the quick, labored breathing behind me. I turned around to look at her. "Think about something else, Delilah."

"How can I, when this is staring at me?" With a small movement of her baton, she gestured to the packed, screaming stadium.

I tried to talk her down. In the back of the band, the drum major caught my eye. He shook his head at me and motioned for me to face forward. But I couldn't abandon Delilah, and Mrs. Baxter was no help. She'd climbed up into the press box to watch the show.

Robert was standing with his trumpet right next to Delilah. He could talk to her without turning his head. "Robert!" I whispered. "Tell Delilah some jokes until we go on the field."

He looked at Delilah, whose sequined bosom rose and fell rapidly, then at me. "Jokes about what?"

"Anything but fainting." I turned around, put my hands on my hips, and grinned my majorette grin.

Behind me I heard Robert say quietly, "A priest, a rabbi, and a majorette walk into a bar." I lost his voice in the crowd noise after that, but periodically I could hear Delilah giggling, which was a good sign. It meant she was still breathing.

The drum cadence began. We marched onto the field—

that is, the band marched, and the majorettes high-stepped. Glancing at Delilah on one side of me, Addison on the other, and the rest of the majorettes lined up perfectly beyond her, I thought we looked pretty cool.

The halftime show was a blur of adrenaline, song after song and toss after toss. I only knew that I performed every routine exactly right. I felt high—almost like I'd been kissing Max.

It was only after we'd marched off the field that I heard the other majorettes whispering. Delilah had managed not to faint, but Addison had dropped her baton four times. And Addison wasn't playing drama queen this time. She was unnaturally quiet.

We stood on the sidelines to watch the home band's show and clapped for them. When third quarter started, we filed back into the stands to sit down, and the game got interesting. Carter threw for a touchdown, and Max kicked the extra point. Our team scored a touchdown, but our kicker couldn't put the ball through the uprights for seven. In the fourth quarter, Max kicked a long, beautiful field goal. Our team made yet another touchdown with yet another missed extra point. I bet our coach was really wishing he had Max for a kicker just then.

It would have disappointed Max and Carter, but I would have loved for the game to stop right there. Our team was winning by two points, but Carter had gotten his touchdown, and Max had proven his worth with his field goal. Everybody could have gone home somewhat happy. But when there were only seconds left on the clock and it looked like there was no way their team could win because they were too far from the end zone, their coach sent Max in to kick a forty-eight-yard field goal, nearly impossible for a high school player. If he made it, they would win by one point.

No pressure.

"Gemma!" someone called above me in the band. I turned around to see Robert in the trumpets, cupping his hands to yell at me. "Is that your guy?"

I grinned proudly and nodded.

"Can he make that goal?"

I nodded again. I had seen Max in action.

Robert cussed. I laughed as I turned back to watch Max.

The crowd had been feisty all game, but that was nothing compared with the roar around us now. As the play clock ticked down, Max performed the ritual I'd seen him do before his last field goal. He stood beside Carter, who would be catching the snap. He counted a pace to one side and a pace upfield to find his position. Just as he was signaling Carter to call for the snap, whistles blew everywhere.

"What does that mean?" Delilah asked impatiently.

“Our coach just iced the kicker,” I grumbled.

“He did what?”

“We had a time-out left,” I explained. “Our coach called it at the last second before Max was going to kick, just to rattle him.”

“I want us to win,” Delilah said, “but that doesn’t seem fair.”

“Max would be the first to tell you that life isn’t fair.” And icing the kicker seemed to have worked. While the time-out ticked away, Max paced up and down the fifty yard line with his hands on his helmet. Carter stood stationary, watching Max and yelling at him. Carter probably wished he’d been a little more supportive of Max during summer practice.

The time-out ended. The teams lined up again. The play clock ticked down. Max stood beside Carter, where the ball would be. He counted a pace to the side and a pace upfield to find his position in relation to the ball. Then he should have signaled to Carter that he was ready for the ball. The play clock showed he was running out of time. Three . . . two . . . one . . . and the referees blew their whistles again.

I groaned. “Max!”

I couldn’t tell what Carter was shouting at Max, but judging from the way he jumped up and waved his arms, he was losing his mind.

“What now?” Delilah asked.

"Delay of game. Max never started the play, so the ball has to move back five yards." As I said this, the refs moved the ball farther down the field. Max walked to his new position with his head down. Now the distance between him and the goalposts was more than half the length of the football field. The crowd booed him.

His own crowd.

The home fans quickly shushed themselves, but I had heard the boo. So had Max. He looked toward the home stands as he walked.

I jumped up. "Go, Max!" I screamed, clapping for him. "You can do it!"

"God, Gemma!" Addison snapped. "Can't you cheer for your own team?"

I almost sat down sheepishly. After all, I was the only person standing up on my side of the stadium, yelling like an idiot. Everybody, and I mean *everybody*, was staring at me.

Including Max. I couldn't see his face behind his face mask, but I felt like he was staring straight at me.

"He is my boyfriend!" I yelled at Addison. Then I turned back to the field and clapped. "You can do it, Max!"

The silence on the other side of the field slowly morphed into a supportive cheer for Max, and the whole stadium roared, louder than before.

"Gemma!" Robert called above me.

I turned around.

"Can he make *that* goal?"

I nodded. I wasn't so sure, but I wanted to be sure. I grinned my majorette grin and turned around to watch Max again.

Delilah slipped her hand into mine and squeezed. "I'm not rooting for them, but I'm rooting for you."

"Thank you," I whispered as Max stood beside Carter. He counted a pace to one side and a pace upfield. The play clock wound down. He signaled to Carter. The ball snapped. Carter caught it neatly and grounded it. Max took a step, dragging his powerful kicking leg from behind him, and connected with the ball. He followed through with his kick and stopped to watch where it went.

The ball sailed fifty-three yards, the crowd noise rising with it. The ball passed exactly through the middle of the uprights.

The opposite side of the field erupted in a huge, booming cheer. We could hear it perfectly because our side was dead silent, except for me, sighing with relief. Their band burst into their fight song.

Max stood motionless, stunned, while Carter jumped up and down. Their entire team, the coaches, and the cheerleaders dashed onto the field to surround Max. Even the student section of the stands spilled over the fence and swirled onto the field, so that I couldn't find Max in the crowd anymore.

"You won the game," Addison said. "Happy now?"

I sat down next to her and tried to think of something soothing to say. I should remind her that she'd ended up with Carter, whom she'd decided she liked better anyway.

Instead, I told her, "I can't be friends with you anymore."

Her blond brows went down, and her lips parted. I could tell she was gearing up to give me a tit-for-tat response. *I can't be your friend either, so there.*

I put my hand on her sequined sleeve to stop her from speaking. "Seriously. I don't say that to be mean, or to get back at you, or to hurt your feelings. But you have hurt my feelings over and over again, for six years. I read insults into everything you say, even when you're trying to be nice." If she ever really was. "That makes me angry, and I do mean things to you in response. I don't like the person I become when I'm around you."

Addison looked down at my hand on her arm. "You're breaking up with me." She didn't sound sarcastic. She sounded sad.

I took my hand off her arm. "I'm not laying blame. I don't want us to have hard feelings against each other or try to get revenge on each other for this. I just think that sometimes two people are meant to be together. We aren't."

I looked nervously at the majorettes around us and the flutes behind us. I didn't want them to hear what Addison was sure to say next above the opposing team's fight song. She would scream that I was being mean and immature by telling her I wouldn't be her friend anymore, all because *I* stole *her* boyfriend.

But she didn't. Instead, she said, "I will always love you."

Before I could stop it, my jaw dropped open.

"And I hate you a little bit too." She reached out and hugged me.

Bewildered, I hugged her back.

She squeezed me once and let me go. "Maybe we could just take a break, then see how we feel."

Normally I would have run away from this proposal, screaming, *It's a trap!* But she was acting so bizarrely mature about all this that I said, "That sounds good."

We would see.

16

As soon as our band played our school's fight song, sounding somewhat mournful under the circumstances, we marched back to the buses and piled on to wait for the trombones to load the instrument truck, and then to drive fifteen minutes home. I was so happy for Max, and hopeful about what might happen next between us. Until I saw the huddle of sequins at the back of the bus, I'd completely forgotten that the majorettes were voting for next year's head.

After all that rigmarole about keeping our noses clean, the vote was casual. Mrs. Baxter handed us each a slip of paper and a pen. We wrote our choice and handed the slip back to her. She counted the votes. In thirty seconds we knew. She walked to the back of the bus and put her hand on my shoulder. "For grace under pressure, we have chosen Gemma."

"Gemma!" the majorettes squealed. All six of them hugged me. I did not make a sound. I squeezed my eyes shut and felt their hugs and considered what this meant. I would be head majorette my senior year. I wouldn't have to try out for majorette again next year. Not that I would mind trying out again. I'd had so much fun performing tonight that I was already planning how I would keep performing after high school. I would try out for majorette at Georgia Tech, and maybe feature twirler.

"The band director will be so pleased," Mrs. Baxter said, bustling away up the aisle and down the front stairs of the bus. The majorettes were telling the whole bus the news too. I saw Delilah several seats ahead, whispering to Robert. Soon he and the trumpets yelled in unison, "Congratulations, Gemma!"

"Congratulations, Gemma," Addison said, squatting beside me in the aisle. "Though I know we're not supposed to be friends anymore."

Her sarcasm didn't bother me, precisely because we weren't friends anymore. That's just how Addison was.

"I'm glad you're going to be head," she said.

"Thank you!" I exclaimed, not hiding my surprise very well.

"I didn't want it," she said. "Not really. This role model shit is for the birds. And I don't like standing out there on the field with everybody watching me. I hated trying out, too."

That's because you dropped your batons both times and boys made fun of you, I thought.

"I might not even go out for majorette next year," she said.

Great. Addison complained that she was bored of Monopoly and wanted to stop playing whenever I started to win. If she wasn't the best at something, she didn't want to try anymore. I could see her quickly devolving into the Bad Majorette, making a joke out of it, even earning a reputation for it and thinking it attracted boys. Which it might, honestly, because boys were weird.

She was part of the majorette line. If she tanked, we all would tank. I could not let that happen.

"It's so early in the season," I said. "We've only had one game. And your drops were at the very beginning, right? Nobody remembered them by the end. We're going to have so much fun this year, and I'll bet you'll want to try out again."

She shrugged. "Maybe."

"You're such a great sax player. You might want to concentrate on that next year and not go out for majorette after all. But gosh, you have until April to decide." I sounded reasonable and authoritative, like a head majorette. Like a teacher. Like a counselor.

Like Max.

All the majorettes jumped and Delilah screamed at a sharp rapping on the emergency exit at the back of the bus. Addison stood up and opened the door.

"Is Gemma home?" came Max's voice.

"Yes," Addison said.

"May I come in and see her?"

Addison backed away in the aisle, making room for Max. Behind Addison, I saw Delilah grin and give me a thumbs-up before she leaned over Robert again.

Max climbed onto the school bus. Impossibly tall, head brushing the ceiling, he closed the door and sat down beside me. He wore track pants and a Japanese T-shirt, and his hair was wet from a shower.

He looked me up and down and back up, eyes slowly making their way from my knee-high boots to my skintight sequined leotard to my purple-streaked hair, and lingering on my tiara. He deadpanned, "You look good."

"You do too," I said truthfully.

He picked up my hand from my lap, his touch sending sparks up my arm. "Carter told me you did something nice for me today."

"Well, it was Carter who did something nice for you," I said. "I only warned him it was coming."

"And you cheered for me."

"I did cheer for you!"

"I heard you." He turned my hand over and put his casted hand on top of it. Looking into my eyes, he said, "I nearly lost it out there, Gemma."

"But you *didn't* lose it, and that's what counts. Obviously it's lucky for us to make out the night before games, and then fight."

He slid his hand up my sequined sleeve to my shoulder. "I don't know about the fight. But if you're willing, I definitely think we should make out every Thursday. At least until the end of football season." He brushed his lips against mine, which sent a little shiver across my chest.

"Or longer," I whispered.

He put his casted hand on my shoulder and set his forehead against mine. "Gemma."

"Yes."

"I have something to tell you."

"I get it. You are making me cross-eyed."

He grinned and backed away six inches. Very clearly, enunciating every syllable, he said, "I want to go out with you tomorrow. On a *date*. With *you*, Gemma Van Cleve. Alone."

"I understand you," I said just as clearly. "I am accepting your invitation to go on a *date*. With *you*. Because I like you in a romantic way."

He laughed and squeezed my shoulders, sending a fresh chill down my arms. "So we're clear on this?"

"If we're not, we have much worse problems than we thought. Where do you want to go for our date? Aren't you working tomorrow?"

"I have to coach my sister's game at eight a.m. Oh God, eight a.m." He looked at his watch ruefully.

"Can I come?" I asked.

"You want to watch me coach soccer?"

"I want to see you as the Justin Bieber of girls' soccer."

He frowned at me. "If you promise not to get jealous. Do you think you can handle it?"

I laughed. "I'll try."

"I don't have to work for the rest of the day, though. There aren't a lot of other games to ref because of the holiday weekend, so I let Carter have them. There's something I need to do around lunchtime, and then I was hoping you would meet me at the park. You know, the park in my neighborhood?"

"How could I forget?"

He turned so red that I could see it even in the dusky bus. He was adorable.

Then he cleared his throat. "Our schools will have football games on the same night for the rest of the semester. I'll never get to see you twirl your baton. When we go to the park, you could show me what you do."

"My majorette routine?" I hid my mouth with one hand so the other majorettes couldn't see as I whispered, "It's kind of dull." I put my hand down. "I could do it for you, though, and then I could do the routine I tried out with."

"Really? Is it different?"

"Yes! I can twirl a baton with my elbow."

"You are kidding." He eyed me like he really thought I might be kidding. I guess it did sound kind of strange.

"I'm not kidding. You'll see." I put my fists on my hips and stuck my chest out proudly. "I can juggle three batons."

"You should be in the circus!"

"I *should* be, if I were surrounded by a lake of fire."

"Tell you what," he said. "You can show me your routines. Then we're going to find a private place behind a rock or up in a tree or something, and we're going to make out. Clear?"

My heart was racing. "Clear."

"And then we can move you to a sidewalk where there are more pedestrians, and you can juggle your batons again. If you collect enough tips, we'll go to dinner."

I raised my eyebrows. "Did you say the reason you were single was that you made girls mad? I don't understand how that could ever happen." I poked him in the ribs, like a girl who wasn't afraid to flirt with her boyfriend.

He flinched. "Me neither."

I patted the tight shirt hiding his hard stomach. "This had better be an athlete's low-fat dinner."

"I will make them hold the butter."

"I like this idea. Oh!"

We both braced ourselves against the seat as the bus rumbled to life and jerked into motion.

"Better go." Max gave me a quick kiss on the lips. "I love you, Gemma. I'm so glad we're together. Finally!"

He paused, looking into my eyes to make sure I'd heard him.

I looked up at him and said, "I love you, too."

His eyes fell to my lips. He put his hand in my big hair and kissed me until the bus bumped into a pothole and he nearly fell down in the aisle.

"More tomorrow," he promised.

Then he jogged up the aisle, toward the bus driver. As he went, people yelled, "That's Gemma Van Cleve's boyfriend!" and "That's the damn kicker from East!" and threw plastic flip folders and tubes of cork grease at him.

The driver stopped and let Max off the bus. He jumped

down the steps and crossed the parking lot. Carter and a group of guys held out their arms and embraced him, slapping him on the back. I watched them walk toward their cars together.

Early Saturday morning I drove my mom to the indoor soccer field to watch the game Max was coaching. I'd mentioned it to her at breakfast and asked if she wanted to come, figuring she'd stay home to work on a charity ball instead. But she'd said yes.

She even folded her hands primly in her lap in the passenger seat of my car, trying very hard not to grab the dashboard in a death grip as she had when she was teaching me to drive. She looked so relaxed that I found the courage to say, "Since we don't have plans for tomorrow or Labor Day, I thought I might drive over to Hilton Head to see Dad. You know, to thank him for the car."

She didn't answer right away. But finally she nodded and said, "You should call him."

"It's short notice," I backtracked. "He might have other plans."

"He might include you in his plans. You're his daughter, Gemma."

I looked over at my mom, hoping she didn't feel betrayed that I wanted to see him.

But her expression was thoughtful. "Or if it didn't work out, you could go during your fall break in October, or any weekend in September when you don't have a band contest." She sighed, leaned back in the seat, and looked out the open sunroof. "It's beautiful over there. You'll love it."

Inside the soccer dome, the huge field had been divided into two smaller fields for kids' games. I recognized Max on one of the fields, surrounded by girls with pink bows in their hair and pink socks pulled over their shin guards. I also recognized his parents sitting on bleachers at one end of the field.

I led my mom in that direction, planning all along how I would introduce her to Max's parents, going over the words in my mind. I didn't want to screw this up. But when we were still several yards away from them, Max's mom jumped up and ran across the plastic turf to hug me. "Gemma! I'm so glad you and Max are together now. Did you see his *kick* last night?" Then she let me go and introduced herself to my mom. She introduced my mom to Max's dad, and we all sat down together. It was impossible to feel awkward around her. I saw where Max had gotten his personality.

"Biscuit?" she asked, leaning across me to offer my mom a plastic container. "They're homemade."

My mom never refused food in a social setting. She rarely

refused it at all. She shocked me this time by putting one hand on her belly and shaking her head. "No, thank you. I'm getting back to my healthy weight, starting today."

I made an effort not to stare at her. I guessed I would be seeing more of her in the gym at our house.

Instead, I stared into the box as Max's mom showed it to me.

"Biscuit?" she asked.

My stomach growled. I'd eaten only a banana for breakfast and argued with my mother over that. She'd said I would be hungry an hour later, and she was right. I was genuinely hungry.

"Thank you." I reached into the box and pulled out a biscuit with ham and cheese. It was soft, salty, and full of butter, and it might have been the best thing I had ever put in my mouth.

Or I could have felt that way because I was already thinking happy thoughts. The game had started. Max paced the sidelines, pointing at the field when the girls looked to him for direction. Sometimes during a big play, he put both hands in his hair, showing off those chiseled arms, and accidentally knocked himself in the head with his cast. I loved watching him engrossed in something he cared about. But I looked forward to our afternoon alone.

A familiar flash of blond caught my eye. Carter, wearing a bright yellow referee's uniform, was running the game on the second field. And on the opposite bleachers, Addison sat watching him. Her mother must have thought Addison couldn't get into too much trouble at a kids' soccer game at eight in the morning. Or she'd met Carter and liked him. Either way, I felt happy for Addison.

She waved at me once, and I waved too. Then I turned my attention back to Max.

In the afternoon I was in the middle of a three-turn with a super-high toss, the baton just missing the branches of a poplar, when I saw Max walking toward me through the park. I impressed myself when I was able to catch the baton despite this distraction. I finished the trick by holding the baton and my other arm out gracefully. "Ta-da!"

He grinned, but he didn't clap for me. He was gripping a bouquet of roses in his casted hand and something else behind his back.

I skipped forward and kissed him hello, consciously trying to slow my heartbeat. I felt totally comfortable around Max, except for that pesky racing pulse.

"For you." He presented me with the bouquet.

I inhaled the scent of the flowers and smiled. "Thank you! Are these the ones Addison tried to send you? You and Carter are into recycled gifts."

"No. And I brought you something else. What I should have given you for your birthday." He brought the monstrosity out from behind his back.

It was not a bear he had built himself. Instead, it was a wildcat he had built himself. It had brown fur, but purple streaked its head, as if Max had gotten into his little sister's watercolors. The wildcat wore a T-shirt like Carter's bear, but this one didn't say I LOVE YOU. It was printed with MARCHING WILDCATS in Max's sharp handwriting. The wildcat also wore a lot of bracelets and necklaces made of crumpled tinfoil beads.

"With my wrist in a cast," Max said, "it's hard for me to do crafts. My sister helped me, in case that wasn't clear."

"I love it." I gave him another kiss. At some point I dropped the wildcat, because he was very bulky, and propped the bouquet against him. Max had all my attention. He deepened the kiss, and I didn't mind. We were alone in this part of the park.

When we took a breath, I rubbed my nose against his. "I need to tell you something. You've said I have a hard time in relationships, so I want to make sure I'm communicating this to you. I don't know what will happen with you and me. In a few hours when we leave, I could walk across the parking lot to my car and get hit by a bus."

Max rolled his eyes.

"Okay, okay, don't do that. This is hard for me. You know, emoting."

Max kept one hand on my waist and held me close, but he deliberately looked at his watch on the other wrist.

"Okay. What I'm trying to say is . . ." I looked into his beautiful dark eyes.

He winced, bracing for it, like he thought I was about to reveal something terrible that would undo three weeks of maneuvering between us.

"You are a very good boyfriend," I said in a rush.

He laughed. "I've been your boyfriend for about sixteen hours."

I tapped my finger on my forehead. "In my mind, it's been longer."

"Mine too." He brushed a strand of purple hair out of my eyes. And he kissed me again.

I kissed him back, then opened one eye to look around. We were still alone. I closed my eyes and kissed him harder, pushing my fingers into his thick hair.

After a few more long, hot, tingling minutes, he broke the kiss. Setting his forehead against mine, he looked into my eyes and whispered, "So far, so good."

Turn the page for a peek at
another sweet and sparkly romance by

Jennifer Echols:

Endless Summer

Sean smiled down at me, his light brown hair glinting golden in the sunlight. He shouted over the noise of the boat motor and the wind, "Lori, when we're old enough, I want you to be my girlfriend." He didn't even care the other boys could hear him.

"I'm there!" I exclaimed, because I was nothing if not coy. All the boys ate out of my hand, I tell you. "When will we be old enough?"

His blue eyes, lighter than the bright blue sky behind him, seemed to glow in his tanned face. He answered me, smiling. At least, I *thought* he answered me. His lips moved.

"I didn't hear you. What'd you say?" I know how to draw out a romantic moment.

He spoke to me again. I still couldn't hear him, though the boat motor and the wind hadn't gotten any louder. Maybe he was just mouthing words, pretending to say something sweet I couldn't catch. Boys were like that. He'd just been teasing me all along—

"You ass!" I sat straight up in my sweat-soaked bed, wiping away the strands of my hair stuck to my wet face. Then I realized what I'd said out loud. "Sorry, Mom," I told her photo on my bedside table. But maybe she hadn't heard me over my alarm clock blaring Christina Aguilera, "Ain't No Other Man."

Or maybe she'd understand. I'd just had a close encounter with Sean! Even if it *was* only in my dreams.

Usually I didn't remember my dreams. Whenever my brother, McGillicuddy, was home from college, he told Dad and me at breakfast what he'd dreamed about the night before. Lindsay Lohan kicking his butt on the sidewalk after he tried to take her picture (pure fantasy). Amanda Bynes dressed as the highway patrol, pulling him over to give him a traffic ticket. I was jealous. I didn't want to dream about Lindsay Lohan or getting my butt kicked. However, if I was spending the night with Patrick

Dempsey and didn't even *know* it, I was missing out on a very worthy third of my life. I had once Googled "dreaming" and found out some people don't remember their dreams if their bodies are used to getting up at the same hour every morning and have plenty of time to complete the dream cycle.

So why'd I remember my dream this morning? It was the first day of summer vacation, that's why. To start work at the marina, I'd set my clock thirty minutes earlier than during the school year. Lo and behold, here was my dream. About Sean: check. Blowing me off, as usual: nooooooo! That might happen in my dreams, but it wasn't going to happen in real life. Not again. Sean would be mine, starting today. I gave Mom on my bedside table an okay sign—the wakeboarding signal for *ready to go*—before rolling out of bed.

My dad and my brother suspected nothing, ho ho. They didn't even notice what I was wearing. Our conversation at breakfast was the same one we'd had every summer morning since my brother was eight years old and I was five.

Dad to brother: "You take care of your sister today."

Brother, between bites of egg: "Roger that."

Dad to me: "And you watch out around those boys next door."

Me: (Eye roll.)

Brother: "I had this rockin' dream about Anne Hathaway."

Post-oatmeal, my brother and I trotted across our yard and the Vaders' yard to the complex of showrooms, warehouses, and docks at Vader's Marina. The morning air was already thick with the heat and humidity and the smell of cut grass that would last the entire Alabama summer. I didn't mind. I liked the heat. And I quivered in my flip-flops at the prospect of another whole summer with Sean. I'd been going through withdrawal.

In past years, any one of the three Vader boys, including Sean, might have shown up at my house at any time to throw the football or play video games with my brother. They might let me play too if they felt sorry for me, or if their mom had guilted them into it. And my brother might go to their house at any time. But *I* couldn't go to their house. If I'd walked in, they would have stopped what they were doing, looked up, and wondered what I was doing there. They were my brother's friends, not mine.

Well, Adam was my friend. He was probably more my friend than my brother's. Even though we were the same age, I didn't have any classes with him at school, so you'd think he'd walk a hundred yards over to my house for a visit every once in a while. But he didn't. And if I'd gone to visit him, it would have been obvious I was looking for Sean out the corner of my eye the whole time.

For the past nine months, with my brother off at college, my last tie to Sean had been severed. He was two years older than me, so I didn't have any classes with *him*, either. I wasn't even in the same wing of the high school. I saw him once at a football game, and once in front of the movie theater when I'd ridden around with Tammy for a few minutes after a tennis match. But I never approached him. He was always flirting with Holly Chambliss or Beige Dupree or whatever glamorous girl he was with at the moment. I was too young for him, and he never even thought of hooking up with me. On the very rare occasion when he took the garbage to the road at the same time I walked to the mailbox, he gave me the usual beaming smile and a big hug and acted like I was his best friend ever . . . for thirty heavenly seconds.

It had been a long winter. *Finally* we were back to the summer. The Vaders always needed extra help at the marina during the busy season from Memorial Day to Labor Day. Just like last year, I had a job there—and an excuse to make Sean my captive audience. I sped up my trek across the pine needles between the trees and found myself in a footrace against my brother. It was totally unfair because I was carrying my backpack and he was wearing sneakers, but I beat him to the warehouse by half a length anyway.

The Vader boys had gotten there before us and claimed

the good jobs, so I wouldn't have a chance to work side by side with Sean. Cameron was helping the full-time workers take boats out of storage. He wanted my brother to work with him so they could catch up on their lives at two different colleges. Sean and Adam were already gone, delivering the boats to customers up and down the lake for Memorial Day weekend. Sean wasn't around to see my outfit. I was so desperate to get going on this "new me" thing, I would have settled for a double take from Adam or Cameron.

All I got was Mrs. Vader. Come to think of it, she was a good person to run the outfit by. She wore stylish clothes, as far as I could tell. Her blond pinstriped hair was cut to flip up in the back. She looked exactly like you'd want your mom to look so as not to embarrass you in public. I found her in the office and hopped onto a stool behind her. Looking over her shoulder as she typed on the computer, I asked, "Notice anything different?"

She tucked her pinstriped hair behind her ear and squinted at the screen. "I'm using the wrong font?"

"Notice anything different about my boobs?"

That got her attention. She whirled around in her chair and peered at my chest. "You changed your boobs?"

"I'm *showing* my boobs," I said proudly, moving my palm in front of them like presenting them on a TV commercial. All this can be yours! Or, rather, your son's.

My usual summer uniform was the outgrown clothes Adam had given me over the years: jeans, which I cut off into shorts and wore with a wide belt to hold up the waist, and T-shirts from his football team. Under that, for wakeboarding in the afternoon, I used to wear a one-piece sports bathing suit with full coverage that reached all the way up to my neck. Early in the boob-emerging years, I had no boobs, and I was touchy about it. Remember in middle school algebra class, you'd type 55378008 on your calculator, turn it upside down, and hand it to the flat-chested girl across the aisle? I was that girl, you bi-yotch. I would have died twice if any of the boys had mentioned my booblets.

Last year, I thought my boobs had progressed quite nicely. And I progressed from the one-piece into a tankini. But I wasn't quite ready for any more exposure. I didn't want the boys to treat me like a girl.

Now I did. So today I'd worn a cute little bikini. Over that, I still wore Adam's cutoff jeans. Amazingly, they looked sexy, riding low on my hips, when I traded the football T-shirt for a pink tank that ended above my belly button and hugged my figure. I even had a little cleavage. I was so proud. Sean was going to love it.

Mrs. Vader stared at my chest, perplexed. Finally she said, "Oh, I get it. You're trying to look hot."

"*Thank* you!" Mission accomplished.

"Here's a hint. Close your legs."

I snapped my thighs together on the stool. People always scolded me for sitting like a boy. Then I slid off the stool and stomped to the door in a huff. "Where do you want me?"

She'd turned back to the computer. "You've got gas."

Oh, goody. I headed out the office door, toward the front dock to man the gas pumps. This meant at some point during the day, one of the boys would look around the marina office and ask, "Who has gas?" and another boy would answer, "Lori has gas." If I were really lucky, Sean would be in on the joke.

The office door squeaked open behind me. "Lori," Mrs. Vader called. "Did you want to talk?"

Noooooooo. Nothing like that. I'd only gone into her office and tried to start a conversation. Mrs. Vader had three sons. She didn't know how to talk to a girl. My mother had died in a boating accident alone on the lake when I was four. I didn't know how to talk to a woman. Any convo between Mrs. Vader and me was doomed from the start.

"No, why?" I asked without turning around. I'd been galloping down the wooden steps, but now I stepped very carefully, looking down, as if I needed to examine every footfall so I wouldn't trip.

"Watch out around the boys," she warned me.

I raised my hand and wiggled my fingers, toodle-dee-doo, dismissing her. Those boys were harmless. Those boys had better watch out for *me*.

Really, aside from the specter of the boys discussing my intestinal problems, I enjoyed having gas. I got to sit on the dock with my feet in the water and watch the kingfishers and the herons glide low over the surface. Later I'd swim on the side of the dock upriver from the gasoline. Not *now*, before Sean saw me for the first time that summer. I would be in and out of the lake and windy boats all day, and my hair would look like hell. That was understood. But I wanted to have clean, dry, styled hair at least the *first* time he saw me, and I would hope he kept the memory alive. I might go swimming *after* he saw me, while I waited around for people to drive up to the gas pumps in their boats.

The richer they were, the more seldom they made it down from Birmingham to their million-dollar vacation homes on the lake, and the more likely they were complete dumbasses when it came to docking their boats and finding their gas caps. If I covered for their dumbassedness in front of their families in the boats by giggling and saying things like, "Oh, sir, I'm so sorry, *I'm* supposed to be helping *you*!" while I helped them, they tipped me beyond belief.

I was just folding a twenty into my back pocket when Sean and Adam came zipping across the water in the boat emblazoned with VADER'S MARINA down the side, blasting Nickelback from the speakers. They turned hard at the edge of the idle zone. Three-foot swells shook the floating dock violently and would have shaken me off into the water if I hadn't held on to the rail. Then the bow of the boat eased against the padding on the dock. Adam must be the one driving. Sean would have driven all the way to the warehouse, closer to where they'd pick up the next boat for delivery.

In fact, as Sean threw me the rope to tie the stern and Adam cut the engine, I could hear them arguing about this. Sean and Adam argued pretty much 24/7. I was used to it. But I would rather not have heard Sean complaining that they were going to have to walk a whole extra fifty yards and up the stairs just so Adam could say hi to me.

Sean jumped off the boat. His weight rocked the floating dock again as he tied up the bow. He was big, maybe six feet tall, with a deep tan from working all spring at the marina, and a hard, muscled chest and arms from competing with Adam the last five years over who could lift more poundage on the dumbbell in their garage (Sean and Adam were like this). Then he straightened and smiled his beautiful smile at me, and I forgave him everything.

About the Author

Jennifer Echols was born in Atlanta, Georgia, and grew up in a small town on a beautiful lake in Alabama—a setting that has inspired many of her books. She has written eight romantic novels for young adults, including the comedy *Major Crush*, which won the National Readers' Choice Award, and the drama *Going Too Far*, which was a finalist in the RITA, the National Readers' Choice Award, and the Book Buyer's Best and was nominated by the American Library Association as a Best Book for Young Adults. Her next two teen dramas, including *Such a Rush*, will appear in 2012 and 2013, with her adult romance novels debuting in 2013, all published by Simon & Schuster. She lives in Birmingham, Alabama, with her husband and her son. Please visit her online at www.jennifer-echols.com.